"Do you want to marry me?"

Willa laughed. "Are you serious?"

"Yeah, why not?" Garrett answered.

"Sorry, Garrett. You've got the wrong woman for that."

"Why? Because of what happened between us?"

"What happened between us besides one night of passion? We were barely adults at the time. But the truth is, I'm never getting married. I'm not going through any of that again."

"No?" He poured himself a shot of whiskey. Then one for her.

She waved it away.

"I don't want to drink alone."

"Well, luckily for you, there's a whole party full of people out there who are drinking."

"I'd rather be in here, drinking with my future wife..."

"Don't bet on it."

"The proposal or the whiskey?"

* * *

A Rancher's Reward by J. Margot Critch
is part of the Heirs of Hardwell Ranch series.

Dear Reader,

Who doesn't love a cowboy?

I don't have any actual cowboys in my life, but ever since I saw a dance routine performed by Las Vegas's *Thunder from Down Under* ("Save a Horse, Ride a Cowboy," indeed), I've been enamored with the rugged masculinity of the handsome rancher.

If you enjoy this novel, you'll be pleased to know there are more sassy heroines and sexy heroes in my Harlequin Blaze and Harlequin Dare books. And while I miss those lines, I am so excited for the opportunity to flex my skills writing for Harlequin Desire. I'm still in shock that I get to write stories in this line, alongside such an incredible roster of authors.

When my editor, Johanna, told me that Harlequin Desire was looking for rancher stories, I was thrilled to create the Hardwells, the elegant, but rustic, ranchers set in the fictional world of Applewood, Texas. I hope you enjoy *A Rancher's Reward*, as well as the rest of the upcoming books in the series.

If you'd like to connect, come find me on Twitter @jmargotcritch. I typically tweet about books, my cats (Hi, Chibs & Otis!), Bravo shows and Jimmy Buffett.

J. Margot Critch

J. MARGOT CRITCH

A RANCHER'S REWARD

HARLEQUIN®
DESIRE™

Recycling programs
for this product may
not exist in your area.

ISBN-13: 978-1-335-58134-1

A Rancher's Reward

Copyright © 2022 by Juanita Margo Bishop

For questions and comments about the quality of this book,
please contact us at CustomerService@Harlequin.com.

Harlequin Enterprises ULC
22 Adelaide St. West, 41st Floor
Toronto, Ontario M5H 4E3, Canada
www.Harlequin.com

Printed in U.S.A.

J. Margot Critch currently lives in St. John's, Newfoundland and Labrador, with her husband, Brian, and their little fur buddies. A self-professed Parrothead, when she isn't writing, she spends her time listening to Jimmy Buffett and contemplating tropical locales.

Books by J. Margot Critch

Harlequin Desire

A Rancher's Reward

Harlequin Dare

Sin City Brotherhood
Boardroom Sins
Sins of the Flesh
Sweet as Sin
Forbidden Sins
A Sinful Little Christmas

Visit her Author Profile page
at Harlequin.com for more titles.

You can also find J. Margot Critch on Facebook,
along with other Harlequin Desire authors,
at Facebook.com/HarlequinDesireAuthors!

For Johanna,

You've been by my side since the absolute beginning, and I couldn't imagine writing this book without you. Your guidance over these years has been invaluable, and I'm so blessed that you're still with me.

One

In heels that were a little too high and pinched her toes a little too much, Willa Statler made her way through the crowded party. She walked past joyous partygoers, dodging those who wildly gestured with their hands and full glasses, weaving elegantly between huddled groups who joked and laughed loudly. None of them paid her any mind. Willa was the event coordinator, and she should be invisible unless there was a crisis of some sort.

Her eyes homed in on an abandoned half-filled glass of red wine that sat perilously close to the edge of a table. Without breaking her stride, Willa reached out and picked up the glass, avoiding a potential disaster. To her left, she noticed a pillar candle in the mantel centerpiece had extinguished. With her free hand, she reached into the small purse that hung over her shoulder, that managed to hold everything she would need for an emergency, should one arise—her cell phone, a pen, bobby pins, stain remover and, in this case, a book of matches. Making herself small in the crowd, she wove her way to the mantel and relit the candle.

Gliding effortlessly through the partiers, Willa made her way to the outer edges of the crowd, to quickly deposit the offending wineglass on the bar, and kept her eyes peeled for any other small details or potential catastrophes to attend to. She sought out Elias Hardwell and Cathy—the soon-to-be Mrs. Hardwell—to make sure they were both still happily enjoying their engagement party. It pleased her to see that they were holding court near the open French doors that led to the patio. They looked happy, but not just that—they *were* happy. If Willa were to pat herself on the back, she'd tell herself that it was a great party for a fabulous couple. Most of the guests were talking, laughing. The drinks were flowing; the food and service were great; the decorations, on point; the happy couple looked just that—all the hallmarks of a good time. Willa had done a bang-up job on this one.

And while that should have been enough to make her happy, it wasn't. In the two years she'd been working as an event coordinator, she'd become one of the best, most sought-after wedding profession- als in High Pine, Texas, the larger town that was close to rural Applewood, where she'd grown up, and which, despite its small size, still managed to be one of the richest towns per capita in the state of Texas. Despite what had happened two years ago at her own wedding—and her self-imposed exile from her hometown—that demand had bled into Applewood's social circles. As good as she was at her job, pulling off the perfect wedding day for a happy couple wasn't her passion. It was just her job. It wasn't her choice that her boss assigned her every wedding that was booked at the event-planning company where she worked. She was good at it—one of the best—but she didn't have to like it.

She looked at Cathy and Elias again, taking in their loving glances and the way they touched. From talking to the couple, she knew that they were madly in love with each other. They were both moving on to their second marriages—Cathy, a divorcée; and Elias, a widower. She hoped they would remain as happy as they were tonight. But realistically, Willa thought with a sigh, *statistically*, around 40 to 50 percent of marriages ended in divorce. She'd seen it happen. Since she'd started as an event and wedding coordinator, that statistic held true among the couples she'd worked with. She'd seen the joy of a wedding day twist and harden into something ugly. Sometimes it took a year, sometimes longer, sometimes... She blinked away the image of Thomas's anger-reddened face and the shocked murmurs of the congregation, as she took a step back from him at the altar, almost tripping on her long train before hiking it up and running back up the aisle as if she had a bus to catch...

Sometimes it took only five minutes after "Canon in D" to realize that the person you'd agreed to marry wasn't the one you should be with.

Shaking her head, Willa forced herself back to reality. She'd been hired to focus on Elias and Cathy and make sure that they had an unforgettable night at their engagement party. It was her job to stay focused on making sure every detail was perfect.

A deep laugh filled the room and drifted over the voices of everyone else and, whipping her head around to find the source, she saw Garrett Hardwell, chatting and laughing with a group. Elias's grandson looked good, and he commanded attention everywhere he went. With his light brown hair combed back and missing his signature Stetson—it was a formal indoor event, after all—he was wearing an extremely well-tailored gray suit, no tie, his white shirt open to reveal a tanned throat. Not that she was staring, of course. It was her job to notice details. Details like how humor caused his eyes to glitter in the room's low light, how his soft, full lips turned upward in a charismatic smile, how the cords of his neck were taut as he said something that made the rest of the group erupt into laughter. For a moment, she imagined skimming her lips over all of him... Just one more time.

"Well, look at the wedding-planner extraordinaire," Willa heard her brother, Dylan, say from behind her, jarring her from those thoughts. "Great party, Will."

She turned quickly so Dylan wouldn't catch her staring at his best friend. "Thanks." She tried to push past the fog of lust that Garrett had caused in her head and tried to focus on the event—an engagement party, a joyous occasion, one to celebrate two people finding each other in a chaotic world and making a commitment to stand by one another, no matter how impossible that idea seemed sometimes. "Everything seems to be going well."

"Because they have the best wedding planner in Applewood on it."

Willa smiled at her brother. No matter what she did, no matter what people said, Dylan always had her back. He always protected her. He was her biggest fan. "Yeah, of *all of* the wedding planners in Applewood." More accurately, she worked out of High Pine—the next town over. "But it's nice of you to say."

"It's true. Elias and Cathy wouldn't have hired you if you weren't the best," he said, giving her shoulder a squeeze. "I just got here. Have you seen Garrett?"

She blinked rapidly at his question. Of course she'd seen him. Every time she was in the same room as Garrett—which hadn't been often in the past ten years—her eyes would instantly gravitate to the man. She raised her hand and casually gestured in his direction, trying her best to seem indifferent to him. "Yeah, he's over there."

As if he knew they were talking about him, Garrett looked over and waved. Dylan waved back but didn't have a chance to join his friend, because, just then, the sound of a metal utensil hitting a fine crystal glass filled the room. After so many weddings, the sound grated up Willa's spine, but she smiled and turned in the direction of the noise and saw it was Elias. She was caught off guard. Elias had told her of his intention to say his thank-yous at the end of the night. Were he and Cathy leaving early? She hated when people altered their plans, but rolling with changes was one of her specialties. She headed in Elias's direction in case he needed anything during his impromptu speech.

With her head on a swivel, keeping an eye out for any potential problems, she hadn't been watching where she was going, and with her shoulder, she brushed against a firm arm. "I'm sorry about that," she said before she had a chance to look up at whom the arm belonged to. When she did, her breath almost caught in her throat. It was Garrett. The spot on her upper arm that had brushed him still felt like it radiated heat.

"It's quite all right, darlin'," he said with an amused drawl.

It looked like he had something else to say, but she quickly moved on. She had a party to keep on track; she couldn't spend her night chatting up one of the guests—no matter how sexy he was. No matter the history between them.

The din of lively partygoers quieted as Elias raised his hand and drew Cathy closer. "We would like to thank you all for coming tonight. But before the night goes on too long, I—we—have an announcement to make." There was a murmur of surprise. What sort of additional announcement could the elder Hardwell have to make at his engagement party?

"While you're all here, I would like to take this opportunity to officially announce my retirement." There was a collective gasp from the audience, and Willa whipped her head in Garrett's direction. As Elias Hardwell's grandson and right-hand man, Garrett seemed just as surprised as everyone else by the announcement. "I've worked my entire adult life with our dedicated team of ranchers to make Hardwell Ranch the success that it is. I'm an old man now," he said to a chorus of well-meaning deniers. "You're all too kind. It's time to pass the work on to the next generation. Cathy and I will be moving to Arizona. It's time for a change. I will be stepping away from the ranch and the business. I trust I'll be leaving it in good hands."

She looked at Garrett again, and he grinned, and she wondered what was going on in his mind. As Elias's second-in-command at Hardwell Ranch, he was no doubt in line to accept his rightful place of leading it. But with the surprise of Elias announcing his retirement and upcoming move, Willa could feel every bit of air being sucked out of the room. Her flawlessly planned party was quickly becoming a disaster. She knew from experience that family gatherings were normally wrought with underlying tension, and sometimes major announcements like a retirement—especially when there was a fortune involved—could cause an uproar. She thought about starting the music up again to keep the party going, but she knew that a man like Elias Hardwell would not take kindly to being cut off; so Willa clenched her fists and prayed that the speech would end soon without any further drama.

Retirement. That word had gotten Garrett's attention. He had never expected that from his grandfather. Even though Elias was getting on in age and had worked hard to build the ranch to the successful, formidable business it was, Garrett had always imagined the old man sticking around until his dying day. Meeting Cathy had changed that, and he couldn't fault Elias one bit. The loss of his first wife, Garrett's grandmother, had deeply affected them all. Their matriarch had never been forgotten, but tonight his entire family had congregated to wish Elias and Cathy a happy engagement.

He'd been enjoying the party that Willa Statler had put together. It had been fun, a chance to catch up with his family, his brothers and all the cousins who had spread throughout the country. But with his grandfather's announcement, Garrett's mind began to race—he didn't like surprises. With his grandfather stepping down, what did that mean for Hardwell Ranch? He'd never had the succession conversation with his grandfather. He didn't think he would sell Hardwell Ranch; but based on his words, did he mean that it would go to his father and aunts and uncles, all of whom had their own careers away from the ranch and were nearing retirement? Was Elias about to announce that he was leaving the business to him? Garrett smiled. He was the only practical replacement. He'd worked the ranch, under Elias's watchful eye, since he was a teenager.

Garrett looked back at his grandfather, who raised a hand, quieting the crowd once more. What else could the old man have to say? "Furthermore," Elias continued, "while I will always be a part of Hardwell Ranch, I don't need to profit from it any longer. You all know that I have enough. So that's why I'll be leaving Hardwell Ranch and all of its assets in the capable hands of my grandchildren."

Grand*children*? Garrett had been expecting to hear his name only, so it surprised him to hear the others included. He looked around the room. His brothers and cousins all wore the same shocked expressions. There were more than a dozen of them, but he was the only one who actually worked on the ranch. He had been Elias's right-hand man for almost twenty years. Was everyone now entitled to an ownership stake in the ranch he'd personally helped build to prosperity? It wasn't about the money, of course, but he didn't exactly want to be put in a position of working for any of them. He watched his grandfather, hoping to catch the old man's eyes so they could have a word in private, but he was clearly enjoying captivating the crowd and dropping these bombs.

"To be entitled to their shares," Elias continued, "each of my beloved grandchildren will have to return to the ranch and work for a period of six months, to work the land and show that they deserve to profit from its operation."

Shocked gasps rang out in the room. But Garrett stood, immobile, watching as his grandfather sought him out in the crowd. He raised his glass in his direction, and Garrett maintained eye contact with him. "And to you, Garrett. You've been my partner and next in command in this business for years, so you're entitled to the controlling share of it… You will solely be awarded fifty-one percent of the ranch—"

"So what? I just have to work here like everyone else? No problem. I've been doing this since I was fourteen."

Elias chuckled, as if humoring him, and Garrett knew he would pay dearly for that interruption. But he had no idea how much it would cost him. "It's a little more than that, I'm afraid. You get a controlling fifty-one percent, but only if you settle down—" Garrett was taken aback; he didn't like the direction this was heading "—fall in love…" His grandfather paused for effect. "And get married."

The room fell silent. Well, maybe it wasn't silent; maybe Garrett just couldn't hear anything else but the blood rushing past his ears or his heart pounding in his chest. He took a drink to quench his now-parched throat. But instead of swallowing it, he gave a surprised cough and almost choked on his champagne. Amused partygoers turned their eyes in his direction, but he managed to maintain his outward composure and swallow roughly past the lump in his throat, even though the fine liquid turned to glass on its way down. Every pair of eyes that looked back at him was rounded; mouths upturned in amused grins. He turned his attention back to his grandfather. "What did you just say?" he asked, his voice hoarse.

The stares turned to Elias, who grinned. "You heard me, Garrett."

The eager partiers, who were all delighted to be part of what should have been a private family moment, turned back to look at him—looking back and forth like they were spectators at a damn tennis match. Garrett had heard his grandfather. But he still couldn't process the words that had been said to him. As Garrett put down his empty champagne flute, his grandfather's words echoed back in his head.

"When's the big day, little bro?" his older brother, Wes—the normally stoic and reserved one—asked, slinging an arm over his shoulder. He'd had one too many glasses of scotch.

Garrett cleared his throat roughly and, ignoring everyone else in the room, faced his grandfather. "Can we talk in private?"

"Of course."

When they were alone in his grandfather's study, Garrett crossed his arms and confronted Elias. "Now, what the blue hell was that?" When it came to work, they were more friends and partners than grandfather and grandson. At this moment, he wasn't sure what category they were in.

Elias pursed his lips, and without a word, he strode to the small bar in the corner of the room and poured each of them a drink. Garrett recognized the bottle as one of the fine aged whiskeys from a nearby distillery that they both preferred. *The good stuff.* He deserved it. Elias handed a glass to Garrett, and they drank together, just as they'd done many evenings after the board meetings and physical field-work were done. But this time, Garrett felt anything but relaxed. Tonight, they watched each other over the rims of the glasses. Garrett was angry—but more than that, he was curious; he wanted insight into why his grandfather had announced what he had.

Elias finally spoke. "So, what is it? Are you angry that your brothers and cousins are all going to be collecting some share of the business?"

Garrett thought about that for a moment. Sure, he didn't think that any of them would take to life on the ranch quite like he had, and he certainly didn't care about whatever share they might be entitled to, especially since he would own a total of 51 percent of the business. Hardwell Ranch raised herds of livestock—sheep and cattle—but what made them so successful was that they also bred and trained championship horses, sought after by people all over the world. There was plenty of money—and work—to go around. His brothers and cousins getting some of the family fortune wasn't of great concern to him. The money was the least of his worries. "Do you really think the inheritance share is what I'm mad about?"

Elias nodded with a grin. "Ah, it's the other condition, I guess. The wedding."

"Yeah, it's that one. Why do I need to get married—a lifelong commitment—when everyone else is looking at only six months of work to get their share? You know I deserve to own this business. My dedication and blood, sweat and tears over the past twenty years aren't enough for you?"

"Garrett, you stayed with me through the years. You've put in hard work physically, day in, day out—but also in the boardroom, helping make the decisions that have kept us on top. That's why you'll have a controlling share. But I can see the path you're going down. The nonstop work... Even though we pay very competent people to manage the place, you're always here and always on call for anything that might come up."

"There's nothing wrong with that," Garrett insisted. "It's how you did it."

"What is your social life like?" Elias countered.

"What does that have to do with anything?" Garrett truly couldn't remember the last time he'd taken a vacation or spent a late night at Longhorn's with Dylan. He dated occasionally, hooked up with women when he wanted, but it had never amounted to anything serious. He'd long ago learned that with long, unpredictable hours that came with running a ranch, women weren't exactly eager to play second-string to horses and cattle.

"I don't want you to spend your whole life with your mind only on the business," his grandfather told him. "Take this opportunity to focus on finding love this year. And when you're successful at that, you'll have controlling interest of the ranch. The love of a good woman, the support of a part-

ner, that's your reward for all of your hard work,"
he added with a wink.

Garrett thought back through the years. His father had never shown much interest in the ranch,
choosing instead to study medicine and open a medi-
cal practice in nearby High Pine. As a child, Garrett hadn't been interested in the things that living
in a bigger town brought and instead spent almost
every weekend on the ranch with his grandparents
and helping with light duties. Out of high school,
he'd started as a ranch hand—nothing glamorous.
He'd spent day and night tending to the livestock,
mending fences, mucking out stables and cleaning
the grain silos before he was even given a chance to
move up in the ranks of the organization to act as
his grandfather's second-in-command, even though
he still spent more time out on the land than inside.
The success—his dream home on the ranch, prize-
winning horses and the rest of his favorite toys—had
always been his reward. Finding a wife had never
been on his priority list. "But why?" he asked. "I
don't need to be married to run this place. Your stipulations don't make any sense."

"Garrett, you work very hard. I see that. But
you're alone. I want you to be happy."

"Don't worry about me. I am happy," he insisted.
Garrett raised his glass and swallowed the rest of the
whiskey. With a pointed look at his grandfather, he
poured himself another finger—then another—of
Elias's aged special-edition spirit. "You're meddling
in my life, and I don't appreciate it."

"Every man needs the support of a partner, a spouse. Not in business but in life. You need someone to share your success with so you don't end up old and alone, like I almost did."

"You didn't always have a partner. You ran the place for twenty years after Grandma died." When he saw the downturn in his grandfather's lips, Garrett regretted his words. Sometimes his mouth was quicker than his brain. He knew that Elias had been crushed when his first wife had passed and that he missed her every damn day.

"And it wasn't easy. I worked so hard, for so long, to fill the void your grandmother's death left in my life. It didn't work." He hooked his thumb over his shoulder, gesturing to the lively party still happening on the other side of the door. "I stayed busy because it was such a dark period in my life. I was waiting for Cathy. Now that I've found her, I'm stepping aside. I want to enjoy the rest of my life, and I'm not going to work myself to death. I don't want that for you either. Don't wait too long to find someone and end up a miserable old man, with just his money to keep him warm."

Garrett stared at his grandfather with a combination of annoyance and admiration. "You're a manipulative bastard," he said with a smile before taking a drink.

The older man smiled fondly, even though his eyes were serious. "You have one year, Garrett," he said, clapping a hand on his shoulder as he walked past. "Find someone to love, and you can run the ranch and tell everyone else what to do with their shares."

"And if I don't get married?"

"Then you get the same share as everyone else, and I put someone else in charge."

That caught his attention. "Who?"

Elias shrugged. "I don't know. Wes, maybe?"

Garrett snorted. He loved his brother, and he was a good man, but he knew that Wes would just as soon divide the land and build oil derricks or a cryptocurrency-mining farm—or whatever the hell it was that he did—than ever run Hardwell Ranch. And Garrett sure as hell would never work for him. "Over my dead body."

Elias winked and opened the door to the study. The music was playing, and the party had livened again; the guests had moved on from the bomb that Elias had dropped. "That's what I thought. You'd better get to work and find your lucky lady."

Left alone, Garrett poured another drink into his glass. He had to find someone to marry? What a ridiculous request. *No.* Garrett shook his head. It wasn't a request. Elias Hardwell didn't make requests—it was an order. And if Garrett wanted his fair slice of his grandfather's fortune, and to run the ranch he'd worked since he was sixteen, he would have to comply. He blew out a frustrated breath. How was he going to find a woman, fall in love and marry her— all in one year? *Damn.* He shook his head. Even if he started looking right now, it would be nearly impossible.

The door behind him pushed open, and he sighed. It was probably Wes or Noah, or one of his cousins, coming in to twist the knife a little, and he wasn't in the mood to talk to anyone.

"Oh, sorry, I didn't realize you were still in here."

It wasn't a member of his family. He turned to face the familiar voice and managed to smile when he saw it was Willa Statler, who was not only his grandfather's wedding planner but also his best friend Dylan's younger sister. The same woman with whom he'd also shared an intense, short and secret night more than a decade ago. That night had been something that he should have put a stop to. But instead, a night with his best friend's younger sister had gone much further than either of them had intended. He'd tried to put it past him, to forget about her, especially after she left town the next day. But that didn't mean that after all this time, he couldn't still feel her lips on his, her soft skin under his fingertips.

Their lives had taken them in entirely different paths, and even though they'd attended some of the same social functions over the years, because of Garrett's dislike of her former fiancé, Applewood's current mayor, Thomas, he had rarely spoken with Willa or even seen her one-on-one. As far as he knew, she now lived and worked in High Pine and spent most of her time there. He'd known that, because she was his grandfather's wedding planner, he would be seeing her around the ranch more; but knowing that hadn't prepared him for the way his chest clenched, seeing her standing in front of him now.

"That's okay," he told her. "I just needed a little quiet."

She nodded. "Well, I'm sorry to interrupt. I just came in to get something for Cathy," she explained, pulling a white binder from the nearby bookshelf. "She already has some ideas for the wedding."

Garrett could make out the words on the spine— "Best Wedding Ever!"—which reminded him of his own predicament. His own wedding was already on the horizon. Talk about your curveballs.

Willa paused and looked at him with a slight tip of her head. "Are you okay? That got pretty crazy out there."

"I'm fine." Held up his glass. "I'm just drinking to forget how my grandfather is interfering in my life."

Willa cringed. "Yeah, I saw that. But why don't you come back to the celebration and worry about all of that tomorrow?"

"Why? Am I ruining the party you worked so hard to pull off?"

She put the binder on the corner of Elias's desk and came farther into the room. Despite everything else that should have been on his mind, he couldn't help but notice how gorgeous she looked. Her blond hair had been twirled into a tight, professional bun; and her knee-length navy blue dress—which brought out the icy color of her eyes—was modest, with long sleeves and a high neckline; but the material still clung wickedly to her trim but curvy body, not leaving much to his imagination. Not that he had to dig deeply into the recesses of his mind to conjure his memories of their time together…

"Maybe," she answered. "God knows it wouldn't help my professional reputation for there to be an *incident* at a party I planned. So, tell me, I need to know—are you *really* okay? Because if not, I can sneak you out of here, and you can go home without anyone noticing."

He nodded, impressed by her talent to assess a situation. "You are good. Thank you for your concern, but I'm fine," he insisted. "The last few minutes have really taken me for a ride, is all."

"I'd say," she said with a laugh that sounded forced. "Applewood's most eligible bachelor is finally going to get married?" She was still laughing, but Garrett couldn't be sure why there were shadows in her eyes—fatigue or something else?

He shrugged. "I guess I have to. I've worked here for too long to have to work for anyone else. This ranch is rightfully mine. If I have to find a wife to show that, then I will."

"I guess you've got some work to do. You know, you can download one of those apps," she helpfully supplied. "It shouldn't be too hard to find someone who will marry you there. Just swipe right—or is it left?"

Garrett looked at the woman in front of him. She was his best friend's younger sister. He'd known her for a long time. Hell, he'd known her longer than most. Back then, she'd been a fun-loving, lighthearted young woman, with whom he'd shared one of the best nights of his life. But there was no way she still re-membered that night as vividly as he did.

Willa, today, was a poised, sophisticated, profes-sional, absolutely stunning woman. So much time had passed since that night. More than ten years. She'd seen a tumultuous relationship and had been unfairly targeted by the Applewood rumor mill. On the flip side, his reputation had been noted for his hard work—and then the nights he'd spent as a younger man, carousing at the local bars, picking up women as the town's most eligible bachelor, had *strangely* gone undiscussed. He'd loved and left a number of women, but that night with Willa so many years ago was never far from his mind.

Back then, he'd been stupid, immature and too worried about how being with her would affect his friendship with her brother, too willing to throw away a good thing in order to sow wild oats. He'd always wondered how his life would have been dif-ferent if she hadn't left Applewood the next morning. He'd never been given another chance with her; the timing had never quite lined up for him. Pushing her away was something he still regretted…

Willa cleared her throat and raised an eyebrow. She'd said something and he hadn't responded, leav-ing far too long a pause between them. He shook his head, clearing his mind free of the distraction of his thoughts. What had she said? Something about apps, swiping right. "I guess you're right."

Then it came to him. It was a stupid idea, maybe; an insane idea, *definitely*; and it had the potential to blow up spectacularly in his face. But still, he said the words. "Do *you* want to marry me?"

Her face was frozen in place for several seconds before she blinked. And then she let out a shocked laugh. "Are you serious?" she asked, her voice shaky.

Was he? The more he thought about it, the more he realized that it wouldn't be the worst thing—would it? His grandfather had told him to get married, but he didn't say it couldn't be a fake marriage. What the old man didn't know wouldn't hurt him... Garrett put on his most charming smile, the one that normally got him everything he wanted. "Yeah, why not?"

Willa folded her arms across her chest, drew her bottom lip between her teeth and chewed. A long-standing habit that he could see she hadn't broken in the past ten years. Although he was now in his thirties, it still had the same effect as it had back then. He itched to take that lip between his teeth and nibble. She was silent for several beats, and she looked away from him. But she shook her head. "Sorry, Garrett," she said, patting his chest lightly with her manicured fingernails. "You've got the wrong woman for that."

"Why? Because of Dylan?" He narrowed his eyes. "Or because of what happened between us before?" In his mind's eye, Garrett could see himself with a shovel, just digging deeper and deeper. Maybe he would soon reach six feet, and he could just lie down dead. Why was he pushing this?

"Garrett, what happened between us, besides one night of passion when we were much younger? It was nice, sure. But we were barely adults at the time."

Garrett could have slapped himself. He felt like an idiot. Of course, she'd grown up. That night had clearly meant nothing to her; meanwhile, he'd thought about her every day. Way to show your ass on that one. He opened his mouth to tell her he'd misspoke— or anything—but she spoke first.

"But, yeah, sure. It's because of Dylan," she told him, clearly avoiding the topic of anything they may have had in the past. "You know how protective my brother is. Explain to him that you want to marry me to get your grandfather off your back. But the truth is, I'm never getting married. I'm not going through any of that again. It's definitely not for me."

"No?" He shrugged and poured himself another shot of whiskey. And then one for her in a second glass. If he wasn't careful, he would end up piss drunk, owing his grandfather an expensive bottle. *And how will I pay for it if I lose the ranch?* he mused while pouring a little more in his own. He offered her the glass, and she waved it away, still clearly annoyed at him. "I can't. I'm working."

"I don't want to drink alone."

"Well, luckily for you, there's a whole party full of people on the other side of that door who are drinking. No need to do it alone."

He contemplated the party in the other room. "I don't really want to be out there," he told her, shaking his head. "I'd rather be in here, drinking all of my grandfather's special aged whiskey with my future wife...?" He held up the glass again and shook it enticingly.

She smiled and took the glass from his fingers but still didn't drink. "Don't bet on it."

"The proposal or the whiskey?"

"Either. Both. Pick one."

"Come on…" he prodded playfully. "I'm just asking you for this one simple thing."

"Not a chance. Take it from me, there is nothing simple about a wedding."

He grinned, but she looked away from him. "Okay, then," he drawled. "By comparison, having a drink with me would be far simpler." She rolled her eyes, but she didn't leave. "Why don't you want to get married, Willa? You were engaged a couple of years ago. Well, you made it to the altar, at least. Isn't a marriage—a commitment—something you want?" He was on dangerous ground, and he could about feel it shake under his feet as he continued to dig deeper, deeper. The alcohol had loosened his tongue. If he'd been more sober, he might have stopped talking and let her return to the party minutes ago. But he wanted to be around her again, to have her to himself for just a little while longer. He looked her up and down. What he'd proposed was a fake marriage—but damn, if the thought of marrying her wasn't becoming more and more appealing to him.

Willa's face scrunched up, and he knew it wasn't from the whiskey. She ignored his comment on what she'd always wanted, and he was glad. Garrett wasn't ready for that conversation tonight. "Ugh. Thomas." She spat out the name of her former fiancé, and Applewood's "esteemed" mayor. "Yeah. That was…"

She seemed to search for the word. "…one of the mistakes that I will always regret. Like I said, I'm not interested in ever again settling down, getting married or any of that nonsense."

"There's a larger story there, right?"

"You've heard the rumors, I'm sure."

"Yeah, I did hear the rumors, but I know that they're just that—rumors. I never did catch the full story."

"I don't believe that for a second. You know how people talk around here."

"Well, thankfully, I don't pay attention to any of that." She rolled her eyes at him, like she didn't believe him. "It's true. I've heard rumblings, but I don't know what happened. I feel like I need to hear it from you, though."

"Trust me, the truth is far more boring."

"I think I'd like to hear it from you anyway."

"Not a chance." She raised her glass to her ruby-red lips—he noted that the color didn't even leave a mark on the crystal tumbler—and finished the rest of her drink, and he did the same.

"Being anti-wedding is an interesting stance for someone in your field," he noted, one eyebrow raised. "Planning weddings and such."

"I'm an event coordinator. I'm meticulous and detail-oriented, so my boss keeps assigning me to do weddings. Despite how I feel about the things, weddings are where the money is, and I'm one of her best at them."

He believed it. She'd always been a stickler for

details, organized and everything else that would make her a fantastic event coordinator. "So you're sure? You really don't want to marry me? You'd be really helping me out of a bind."

"I'm afraid not, Garrett. It's never going to happen."

He took one last shot. "I'll pay you." He dug the imaginary hole a bit deeper.

She jolted back, and he knew that had not been the right offer. "Excuse me? I'm not for sale."

"There's a whole lot of money coming to me if I fulfill my grandfather's wishes. If you marry me, I'll give you whatever sum of money you think is fair."

She sighed, and he feared that her patience was wearing thin. He was running out of time with her. "You can't buy me, Garrett."

"Everyone has a price."

"Not me." She hooked her thumb over her shoulder. "In fact, maybe someone out there will marry you. Although, between you and me, I'd wait until after your grandfather's engagement party to propose to someone else. You don't want to steal their thunder at their own party." She put down the glass and turned away, but he reached out and caught her wrist, stopping her.

He released her hand and took a step closer. Too close. Only a few inches of charged air separated them. "I don't know about thunder, but there's still some lightning between us."

Willa's surprised gasp as her lips parted was short, and Garrett saw the almost imperceptible way she leaned forward. He did the same. He inhaled the light scent of her perfume, saw the glossy glisten of her lipstick. He lowered his head, and she rose to meet him. He could feel her breath on his lips, but then she pulled back.

"That was really cheesy, you know."

In an attempt to look more casual than he felt, he shrugged. "A guy can try." He finished his drink, vowing to make it his last for the night, lest he get himself into even more trouble. "Well, if you aren't going to kiss me, marry me or tell me your deep, dark secrets, I guess I'd better get out there."

She laughed. "I'll see you, Garrett. Good luck. You're going to actually have to find the love of your life on your own, I guess."

Two

The next morning, Willa tapped her fingers impatiently on the countertop of the small shared work kitchen while she waited for her espresso to finish pouring. When the last of the coffee sputtered into her cup, she didn't bother with any of her usual sugar or cinnamon before she picked it up and drank it all in one gulp. The still-hot liquid burned her throat, and she let out an inelegant squawk before putting the cup back under the dispenser and putting another pod of espresso in the top of the machine. This was definitely a two-double-espresso kind of morning.

As she waited for her second caffeine fix, she looked around the open-concept office space that housed the small but in-demand event-coordination company she worked for. Each corner was occupied by a desk of one of her three coworkers, while their boss Miriam's desk sat in front of a set of large windows that showcased scenic High Pine's bustling downtown.

Miriam came into the small break room with a smile. "Willa, how is your morning going?"

Willa stifled a yawn. "It's fine. I just need some coffee before I start my day."

"Late night at the Hardwell engagement party?" Miriam asked.

"Sort of," she responded. Despite the fact that all the ranchers who'd attended the party had early mornings in front of them, it had gone on late into the night. The event had gone off without a hitch, though, and she'd managed to avoid Garrett the rest of the night—or had he been avoiding her? As if the late night at Hardwell Ranch hadn't been enough, she'd spent a sleepless night mulling over Garrett's non-proposal proposal. And it had nothing to do with the way he'd touched her the night before, and absolutely nothing to do with their near-kiss. Although, when she closed her eyes, Willa could feel the way her body fit against his, and plucking memories from more than a decade ago, she could feel his lips against hers. Like they always did, those thoughts had led to the long, detailed memories from that night, which were followed by the regrets she felt about leaving town for college so abruptly, being too afraid to even consider giving them a chance. *Well, that's the thing about regret,* she told herself, *you have to let it go or become burdened with it.*

Instead, it seemed that she was just adding to her list of regrets instead of letting them go anywhere.

"I just received a call from Cathy," Miriam said with a smile, pulling Willa back into the real world. "She was absolutely gushing about the party last night. I can't wait to see pictures. You must have done a fabulous job."

Willa picked up her second espresso and took a moment to let it cool this time before drinking some of it. "Thank you," she said. "Elias and Cathy are such a great couple—fabulous to work with." That was the truth. She loved clients like them, who made the job worth it. Willa might not love the wedding-planning aspect of the job, but she wouldn't dare complain about it to her boss. She would do her best, no matter the task.

Together, they made their way to the office area, where Mallory, another coordinator at the company, was seated at her desk.

Mallory looked up. "Those came for you," she said, her lips turned upward in a smile as she pointed to Willa's desk on the other side of the room. Willa turned and her mouth dropped when she saw the bouquet that sat in a glass vase on her desk.

"I signed for it," Mallory supplied. "There's a card."

"It must be from Cathy and Elias," Miriam guessed.

"You get all the good clients," Mallory said with a playful roll of her eyes.

As Willa got closer, she could see the bright yellow of the buttercups, almost reflecting the sunlight. But there were also delicate yellow roses and light green guelder roses. It was a stunning arrangement, but her eyes caught on the buttercups, and they stirred up memories of long ago. They'd always been her favorite. She'd often picked small bouquets of them to decorate her room in whatever foster home she and Dylan had found themselves in. They'd always been a small comfort for her.

It brought her back to that day, as afternoon became evening, she and Garrett had spread out on a blanket among the wildflowers in a secluded, grassy spot, next to a running stream on the Hardwell property, looking up in the sky, talking, daydreaming, which led to a warm night, the taste of strawberry wine and the smell of worn leather from their boots. She knew immediately that the flowers weren't from her clients. "It's not from Cathy and Elias," she said, plucking the card from the bouquet. She opened the envelope, and rolled her eyes at what it said: *Marry me, Buttercup*, written with a familiar hand.

"So who's it from?" Miriam asked.

She quickly folded the card and put it in her desk drawer. "Just an old friend," she explained.

"Must be some friend," Mallory muttered. "Such a gorgeous arrangement."

She closed her desk drawer and admired the bouquet. "Yeah, he certainly is…" As the memories hadn't been far from her mind, she recalled the night before. Garrett had looked down at her with those green eyes—that cocky, amused half smile—and her heart rate had ratcheted up a couple dozen notches.

Even though she knew it was just a ruse, a fake re-lationship to appease an old man, how close she had come to saying, "Oh God, yes!" and throwing her-self into his arms when he'd asked her to marry him. Willa was quite pleased with how cool she'd played it. The guy was as gorgeous as any Hollywood hunk, but there was no way she was going to set herself up for that kind of pain, no matter how gorgeous he was, no matter how nicely he asked, no matter how much money he offered…

Miriam walked across the room to her own desk and pulled several folders out of her top drawer, handing one stack to Mallory and the others to Willa. "I've got the dossiers on your next four clients. All weddings. They should keep you busy until late next year."

More weddings. "Great," Willa said, feigning en-thusiasm. "What about all of the other events we have lined up?" Conventions, graduation parties, rodeo fundraisers, balls and galas all made up the area's social calendar. Anything would be better than spending the next two years consumed with the finer details of weddings, which left her with far too many memories of her own failed one.

"I've given those to Mallory," Miriam said.

"You have such an eye for the intricate details of a wedding—and what can I say?" Mallory offered. "You're so much better at those details than I am."

What, should I just be intentionally bad at my job to get the projects I want? Willa asked herself, but she would never voice those words to either her boss or her coworkers. But with Miriam and Mallory looking at her, she realized that she'd been quiet for far too long. Miriam, her own wedding planner, had taken a chance on her when she'd shown up in High Pine without a job or a place to stay, her wedding updo still intact. Willa always prided herself on doing the best job she could. Even if weddings dredged up some terrible memories for her, she had to suck it up, take care of business and do her job.

"Thanks," she said, taking the folders from Miriam. "I'll get cracking on these." She sat at her desk and looked over the informative packets for her upcoming clients—information about happy couples vowing to spend the rest of their lives together. But she knew it didn't always work out that way. They all seemed like nice people, some she recognized from town and some she didn't, but Willa just couldn't muster up any excitement for their future nuptials—and that wasn't a good sign of an event coordinator. *No, you're a wedding planner*, she told herself.

She pushed the folders aside and picked up her small espresso cup. Regretfully, the remaining amount of the brew had turned too cold, but she drank it down anyway. She took out her phone, initially to find the pictures that she'd taken at the party to send them to Miriam; but then she scrolled even further back until she found the one she was looking for.

She could feel the wistful smile on her face as she looked at the run-down sixteen-room mansion situated on the town line between Applewood and High

Pine. For years, since she'd learned that it had once been owned by her family, it had been her dream to buy the place, renovate it and turn it into an inn. She'd told Thomas, her ex-fiancé, and after their failed wedding day, he'd bought the property, and told her that if she wanted it, she could buy it from him, right after he jacked up the price. And of course, after spending most of her savings on the wedding that she'd run away from—he'd screwed her over on that too—she certainly couldn't afford to buy the place now, not to even mention the renovation and start-up costs.

She put down her phone and turned back to the folders of her upcoming clients. She would just have to keep working, keep saving. But distracting her was the bouquet of flowers that sat on the corner of her desk. Again, Garrett's absolutely absurd offer echoed in her head: *Marry me, Buttercup.* He'd even offered to pay her—something she'd thought insulting the night before. Now she knew that Garrett's money would be a life-changing thing. She could buy the old property, quit the job that made her miserable and do what she wanted with her life.

She remembered the heat that had sizzled between them the night before. He'd taken her hand, pulled her close. And she'd been transported back to the time they'd spent together years ago on a blanket under the stars. She'd fallen for him, but he'd pushed her away, unsure of how Dylan would react to them being together, and not wanting to be tied down with a girl who was leaving town for college anyway.

It had broken her heart at the time, but those memories still had the ability to light her core on fire. No other man had been able to make her feel like Garrett had. She had never been able to forget it. Since that night, Willa hadn't fared better in any of her relationships. Sure, she'd dated, kept it casual with men to protect herself. But several bad breakups had hardened her, and after the Thomas debacle, she'd decided that maybe the long-term commitment she'd sought from Garrett all those years ago wasn't for her. Since the failed wedding, she'd kept to herself and stayed away from men.

She'd always thought about that night and what could have been—if she hadn't gone to Denver for college early, or if he hadn't pushed her away. Did he wonder the same things? Did unanswered questions and unquenched desire keep him up at night?

No sense dwelling the past, though. It had probably been for the best—how things had worked out between them. She certainly didn't have the time or energy to devote to a serious relationship. She looked at the dossiers belonging to her happy clients, before turning her attention to the old property she wanted more than anything, and then it came to her. Maybe Garrett had been right. Whether she'd agreed the night before, or not, he'd presented her with a way for both of them to get what they wanted. She plucked a buttercup from the bouquet and twirled it between her thumb and forefinger.

Marry me, Buttercup.

* * *

Garrett slid his hand over the horse's coat, the golden hair silky under his fingers. "How's she doing?" he asked Dylan.

Dylan gave the mare an affectionate pat on her neck. "She's great. Vet just left. She said in a few weeks, we might be able to take her for a short run."

"We don't want to rush anything with her."

"Of course not."

Garrett smiled and patted the mare, who nuzzled his cheek in response. The horse had been a race-horse, born at Hardwell Ranch and trained at one of their facilities. She'd fractured her leg in compe-tition. When her owner had mentioned putting her down, Garrett couldn't let that happen. He'd bought the injured horse outright, and she was now on her way to making a near-miraculous recovery. She would never race again, but with proper rehabili-tation under the careful eye of the town vet, Daisy, Garrett and his ranch hands would make her com-fortable for the rest of her life. "That's good news."

"Some party last night," Dylan said as they slowly brought the mare back to her stable.

Garrett grimaced at his friend. He'd woken up that morning with a hangover unlike any he'd had since his early twenties. He had his grandfather's whiskey and then the many beers with Dylan—the two of them alone on the patio, away from the rest of the party—to thank for that. As the party went on around them, he and Dylan had discussed every option available to Garrett. Every option besides marrying his best friend's younger sister, that is. That one strangely never came up.

As Dylan got the horse situated in the stable, Garrett turned and surveyed the acres of land before him. "I know we were too busy with my problems last night and didn't really get into yours," he called to Dylan. "But how do you feel about everything? You manage this place. You'll be getting a lot of extra help here for a while when my brothers and cousins show up."

"A whole lot of Hardwells here on the ranch? At least there will be enough work to keep them busy. But I know your brothers and cousins, and how soft they've turned out. I don't know how much help a lot of them are going to be."

Garrett laughed, picturing the dozen or so relatives, who would, no doubt, be more in the way than actually helping.

"And you aren't looking forward to giving them a lot of the grunt work, right?"

"Now, why would I do that?" he asked, laughing. "But someone's going to have to muck the stables every day, right? It's certainly not going to be me."

"If we're being honest, I'm not sure you've mucked one in years. Not that you don't pull your weight, of course."

"You're one to talk. I'm pretty sure the only time we see you this far afield is to tell people what to do." Dylan laughed and shoved Garrett's shoulder. It was all in good fun, of course. He'd worked on the ranch as long as Garrett had and had since become manager. Dylan was Garrett's mainstay, his oldest friend and greatest support. They'd been through so much together. While it had been a long time since either of them had done much of the grunt work, they were kept busy in other areas of ranch life.

Garrett laughed and, thrown a little off-balance from his friend's good-natured shove, regained his footing. If any good were to come from Elias's ridiculous stipulations, it would be watching his brothers and cousins, who had all spread far around the country and taken such varied paths in their lives, work on the ranch every day for a six-month period. It would be a real culture shock, a learning curve for many of them. He looked at Dylan's slick grin as he, no doubt, was picturing Garrett's *city boy* brother, Wes, hauling hay bales and mending fences. Or his younger brother, Noah—more content left to his etchings in his beach house in the Keys—treating leather saddles. Garrett knew that they would have a bit of fun with them.

"So I guess the next engagement party will be yours, huh?" Dylan remarked, nudging Garrett in the ribs with his elbow as he passed. "Any idea what you're going to do yet?"

Removing his hat and pushing his hair back before replacing the hat again, Garrett sighed. "I don't know." He thought about the flowers he'd sent to Willa's office. He wondered what her reaction was. He'd impulsively asked her to be his bride, but the more he thought about it, the more appealing the idea was. It was too bad she hadn't accepted. Maybe he could still persuade her yet. "I guess I'll have to do something. I know Elias isn't going to change his mind. He's firm on the demands and set on seeing me settle down someday soon."

"You got that right. What's your plan?" Dylan asked. "Ask the next pretty young thing you find?"

"Willa suggested I give the dating apps a try."

"Just swipe right?"

"I've never had to resort to those things before. And I doubt it's the right forum for a marriage proposal."

"Your bio can read: *rich rancher with all of his own hair, who doesn't scratch or spit, looking for wife to help him become even more rich.*"

He scoffed. "Sounds unlikely."

"How about the old-fashioned way—actually finding a woman and dating her until you fall in love?"

Garrett thought back to the dates he'd had in the past. While he'd had sexual chemistry with many women, that didn't always translate into a romantic match. He'd found some dates to be too flighty, too conservative, too shallow, too sweet, too intense. Good or bad, too much of any trait wasn't always a positive. "I don't have time for dating. I want this done as soon as possible, before Wes or Noah owns this place."

"That'll be the day. Maybe Elias is bluffing about the whole thing," Dylan suggested.

Garrett shook his head. "He wasn't. His lawyer arrived at eight this morning with the paperwork.

He might be a crazy old man, but his demands are legally binding. What I need is someone I like—it doesn't even have to be love—someone I have chemistry with, and someone I can trust not to screw me over." Even as he said the words, Willa's image sat in the center of his mind. "Man, if only Willa had accepted my proposal. That could have saved me a lot of trouble."

"Willa?" Dylan asked, surprise at the mention of his sister. Then he snorted. "Yeah, that'd be the day. That'd also be the day I kick your ass for going after my little sister."

Garrett knew his instincts had been right on that one. Dylan would be pissed if he found out what had gone down between him and his younger sister; that was why he could never find out about the night they'd shared. "Yeah, I figured as much. What would be ideal would be to find a woman and make an arrangement with her. Make her an offer. Then it's not a marriage but a business deal."

"Think Elias will fall for that?"

"I don't know. The old guy is pretty shrewd." He sighed.

"I guess for the time being, you'll have to go out and find a wife the way men have been finding women for generations around here."

"Sounds like we're going to Longhorn's, then," Dylan said, referring to the one bar in Applewood. The country-and-western bar where everyone in town went to hang out and let loose.

Garrett sighed and nodded in confirmation. "Yeah. Longhorn's."

Garrett's phone rang in his back pocket, and he pulled it out. He didn't recognize the number displayed, but he answered.

"H'lo?"

"Garrett?" He may not have recognized the number, but he would know the voice anywhere. He cast a look at Dylan, who was busy with the horse. He didn't want to reveal to his friend that he was talking to his little sister.

"Yeah, what's up?"

"This a bad time?"

He walked away from Dylan, allowing himself some privacy. "No, not at all. I'm just doing some work. What can I do for you?"

"I've been thinking," she told him.

That got his attention. "Really?"

"Yeah, I'm coming to Applewood to go over some things with Cathy this afternoon. I was wondering if you'd like to get together."

"Why?"

"I don't really want to get into it on the phone," she said.

"Well now I'm intrigued." His voice dropped to a whisper. "You calling to tell me that you'll marry me?"

"How about you meet me for dinner and we'll go from there?"

In his mind, Garrett pictured them both sitting in front of a romantic dinner to discuss the finer points of their deal. "Okay, where should we meet?" he asked.

"Patsy's Diner," she said. "At six."

"Patsy's—not exactly high-end."

"It's good food, though."

"You got that right."

"So, you'll meet me there?"

He looked over his shoulder at Dylan, who wasn't paying him any mind. "It's a date."

Three

After her meeting with Cathy, Willa pulled into the small gravel parking lot of Patsy's Diner. Even though Applewood was home to some of the country's richest ranchers, who could certainly afford more luxurious restaurants, there was something about Patsy's inexpensive, delicious food and the nostalgia of the diner that kept the place busy every day. Willa hadn't been there since she left Applewood two years before, but just thinking about one of Patsy's cheeseburgers made her mouth water. She could travel near and far, but she hadn't been able to find a burger that even touched it in quality.

She walked into the diner, and the aroma alone was enough to transport her to the days of her youth, when she'd worked as a waitress, saving money for college and to finally get out of town. She looked around the crowded diner, wondering if she should have picked a less-public place for her meeting with Garrett.

Then she saw him seated at a far booth. His back was to her, but she could see his reflection in a wall mirror. Thankfully, he'd been able to secure a table that would give them a little privacy for the conversation they needed to have. *Privacy in Applewood? Good luck*, she thought to herself, feeling the eyes of almost every patron on her.

Garrett was looking down at his cell phone as she approached and didn't seem to notice her as she got closer, and was able to see what was on his screen. She stopped when she noticed what he was looking at. He was scrolling through her pictures on one of her social media profiles. His thumb hovered over a picture of her lounging on the sand on a recent beach vacation to the Gulf Coast.

"See anything you like?" she asked.

Startled, he whipped his head back to see her. "I was just—"

"That striped bikini is one of my favorites."

He smiled at her and looked down at his phone one more time. "It looks good," he said. "I might have double-tapped on that one."

As Willa took a seat opposite him, he stood, ever the gentleman, and put his phone into his jacket pocket. "Howdy," he said.

"Hi."

"Are you hungry?"

Having to get to her early-morning meeting with Cathy, she'd skipped breakfast and had only a protein bar for lunch. "I'm starving, actually. I've had a cheeseburger on my mind, all day," she told him. "It's all I could think about."

"Well, you're in luck," he told her, handing her one of the laminated menus. "Cheeseburger is still on the menu."

Not only did Patsy's still sell it but the menu itself also looked like it hadn't been replaced or updated since her days behind the counter there. Somehow, the menu items and the prices had remained the same. "Things never change."

She put down the menu and looked up at Garrett to see that he was already looking at her. But before they could speak, Patsy herself came to the table. "Well, isn't this the be-all, end-all?" she exclaimed, marveling at the two of them. "Willa Statler. What brings you back here, and with this handsome stranger? Garrett Hardwell, it's been far too long since I've seen your face around here."

"Hey, Patsy," Willa said warmly. "I don't get back in town much," she explained, leaving off that it was mostly by choice. "I'm just meeting Garrett here for dinner."

"And Garrett, that's no excuse for you. Where have you been keeping yourself?"

"I've been busy. I know I should come in more often."

"You certainly should. And both of you are here together?"

"We're just having a quick meeting over cheese-burgers," Willa said.

"Not too quick, I hope. I was hoping you were here because Willa's going to be your new bride."

"What?" Willa squawked out the word, at the same time Garrett said "Excuse me?" How could Patsy possibly know what they were meeting about?

Patsy looked down at Garrett. "I heard about what your grandfather pulled at the engagement party. Re-tiring, and then making sure you take a wife." She chuckled. "It must have been priceless."

"I guess word spreads fast," Garrett said, roll-ing his eyes.

"Like wildfire," Willa agreed, knowing all too well.

Patsy laid a hand on each of their shoulders. "Well, it's lovely to see both of you. What can I get for you?"

"I'm going to get the fully loaded cheeseburger with french fries. And an extra-thick chocolate shake," she added.

When Patsy looked at Garrett, he nodded. "That sounds perfect. I'll have the same."

They thanked Patsy, and she headed back for the kitchen. When she was out of earshot, Garrett grinned. "I don't know the last time that woman waited on a table here."

"Yeah, even when I worked here as a teenager, she'd given up waitressing to focus on the other parts of the business. You just know she came out here to check us out and ask questions."

"You think so?"

"Of course. I have to level with you, Garrett. You've had your back turned, but people have been looking at us since I came in." She dropped her voice to a whisper. "There's a table of women a few tables over who won't stop gawking."

Garrett sneaked a peek at the offending table, then turned his attention back to Willa. "I guess that's because we make a great-looking couple."

She knew it was true. But she wasn't here to be the center of gossip again. She had to keep him focused. "But we aren't a couple," she pointed out.

He reached across the table and put his hand over hers. "Not yet. But soon, right?"

She let herself enjoy the warmth of his touch for a moment and take pleasure in the embers that he stoked within her before pulling her hand back. She couldn't let herself be affected by him. If she was going to do this, it wasn't going to be because she had feelings for him. It was going to be a financial agreement and nothing more. "Certainly not yet."

"Well, we've got to give the people something to talk about, right?"

"If we don't end up on the front page of the *Applewood Tribune*, I'll be surprised."

"That sounds a little extreme. Sure, people are interested now, but it's only because of who my grandfather is, and word's gotten out about his ridiculous demands for his inheritance, that's all." He paused. "And I'm sure we'll only get a brief mention on page four." His grin held boyish charm that she found hard to resist.

"You think that's it—your grandfather? And it has nothing to do with you being the town's most eligible bachelor, right? Or its biggest former playboy?" She paused, lifting one side of her lips in a lopsided smile. "Or could it be the fact that I ran out on my own wedding in a dramatic fashion and have rarely been seen in town socially since. And now I am here with you."

"I think you're obsessing a little. Your wedding was more than two years ago. People surely don't still care about that, do they?"

Willa sighed. She hadn't wanted to get into the topic with him. In fact, she hadn't wanted to discuss it with anyone. But in Garrett's company, it was so easy to spill everything. "Every wedding I coordinate, every wedding I attend, the closer it gets to Applewood. There are always whispers and jokes, and people who even come to me with their questions and stupid comments—*Thankfully, the bride is still here, hey, Willa?* It's like people hire me just to humiliate me."

"People don't actually say those kinds of things," he said, before leaning closer. "Do they?"

In response, she rolled her eyes. "I wouldn't have said it if it wasn't true. I wish they didn't. But seriously, have you actually met anyone who lives in Applewood? If there's a town that thrives on gossip more than this one, I'd hate to see it."

"Yeah, I've noticed how people react to me since

the party. Like I'm under a microscope. So yeah, I guess I understand the kind of thing you're talking about. That has to be terrible."

"It is."

He was silent, and Willa could just imagine that he was reflecting on the stories that had surfaced about her after her failed wedding. Leaving her fiancé at the altar. She'd run out of the wedding still holding on to her bouquet, the filmy veil still attached to her hair. "I don't know why you did what you did," he started, confirming that she'd been right about his train of thought, "but I know there must be a reason. There's more to the story than any of us know."

"Yeah," she said quietly. "There is."

"I wasn't at your wedding, but I've heard about it."

"Sorry about the lack of invite. I didn't have a lot of control over the guest list."

"Don't be sorry. I can't imagine many people would invite someone they'd slept with to their wedding ceremony." His head was lowered, but he looked up at her, his eyes smoldering. And just like that, the mood at the table shifted. And she was right back there—the grass, the wildflowers (buttercups), the stream, the shooting stars, Garrett next to her, then on top…

Before she could respond, Patsy returned with their milkshakes. She placed each of the frosted glasses in front of them. It had been years since Willa had had one of Patsy's milkshakes. While she was with Thomas, he'd made her so concerned with watching her waistline and tracking her calorie intake that she'd forgotten about the cold, thick, creamy treat she'd loved as a younger woman. Revulsion rode over her in a wave, like it did every time she thought of her ex. How dare he make her feel like less of a woman? She would never again let a man determine her worth.

She looked up and saw Garrett watching her expectantly, waiting for the first taste to be hers. Willa put her lips around the straw and drank. It was delicious and exactly how she remembered it. When she looked up again, she saw that Garrett still had his eyes on her, his own milkshake remaining untouched.

"What were we talking about?" he asked her.

They had been talking about her disaster of a wedding, and that he understood not wanting to invite him—her former lover—to the ceremony. But she wouldn't dare return to those topics. "We were talking about feeling like you were under a microscope, with everyone knowing you needed to marry." That would get them back on track to the business at hand.

His eyes narrowed, as if he wanted to go back to the last thing he'd mentioned. But instead of refuting what she'd said, he nodded. "Right. That's why I need some help with this. I can't be expected to find the right woman on this timeline, and I can't lose control of the ranch."

She took another sip of milkshake, and the drink was smooth going down her throat. "You asked me right away at the party. Put it in terms of a business arrangement. Why don't you just put your time and energy into a real relationship?"

"I could. There's only one problem with that, though."

"What's that?"

"I'm not looking for a wife."

"But—"

"I'm not looking for any kind of long-term commitment here. I want to be married long enough to fulfill the commitments to my grandfather. But I have no interest in a relationship or any of the trappings that come along with it. You, of all people, must understand that."

"Do I ever? That's obvious, given my past. But why don't you want a relationship?"

"Come on. You're Dylan's sister, we go way back. You've been around the ranch long enough to know what goes into running it. The work, the long hours. I don't have time to focus on making a woman feel like she's number one in my life—when that privilege will always belong to Hardwell Ranch. What woman would want to play second fiddle to horses and cattle?"

"That's fair."

"So that's why I need a fake wife."

Willa nodded and took another sip of milkshake to allow herself time to compose herself. She swallowed the smooth chocolate past the lump that had formed in her throat. In her past relationship, she had been the woman who had to come in second to her fiancé's career. Until it was time to schmooze at a formal event or entertain prospective voters for dinner, Thomas had all but ignored her and put his needs and wants ahead of hers. When she'd gotten out of that relationship, Willa had promised herself that she would never put herself in that type of situation again. And here she now was, thinking about marrying someone who all but vowed to do the same thing. Although, as she thought of her future and the money he was offering, she was doing this for her. She just needed to stay focused on that and not the fire that Garrett managed to stoke within her with only a look.

"I'm in," she said.

He smiled. "I know you are."

"Awfully confident, aren't you?"

"I was hoping that's what you would say. You didn't have to make me wait so long, though. What made you change your mind?"

"You've been my brother's friend for as long as I can remember. You're in a bind, and I wanted to help you out." For the moment, she left out that she was also interested in whatever figure he would offer her in return for her favor.

"You know, I was feeling a bit deflated when you said no at the party. I thought in that moment you were the answer to all of my problems."

"Why did you pick me?" she asked. "There's no shortage of women in Applewood."

"Well, I know you're a good person, and I can trust you. Despite our history, we won't have to worry about developing feelings in this situation, because neither of us wants a real relationship. You were right at the party—we've put all of that past stuff behind us. Because that's what I need. It's a business arrangement and nothing more. How does that sound to you?"

"I agree." She'd told him that she'd put their past behind them, and she thought she had. But being around him was testing her resolve. There was an obvious connection between them, and she just had to be strong. If this was going to go forward as a business arrangement, she would have to keep it as professional as possible.

"So how exactly is this going to work?" she asked. "We just go to the courthouse and get married, followed by a quick annulment?"

He shook his head. "I'm afraid it's not going to be that easy," he told her. "Elias was very specific. He needs to be convinced by the relationship. We can't just come out and announce that we're engaged right away." He took another pull from his straw. "We also have one year to get married. That way, we can announce that we're dating now, and it gives us a year to make it look legit. I know that Elias won't fall for it otherwise. Us reconnecting at the party gives us the perfect excuse to start 'dating.'" He used his fingers to make air quotes around the word.

It was unbelievable. Elias had covered every base to make sure his grandson entered a wedding agreement. She laughed. "You have to admit how ridiculous this sounds. This can't be legal, can it?"

Garrett laughed as well. "According to Elias's demands, I don't have to get married—I have the freedom of choice. But, of course, we know that *freedom of choice* doesn't mean *freedom of consequences*. The consequence, in this case, is that I don't inherit the ranch."

"A year," Willa said, just realizing the implications of what she was agreeing to. She hadn't been sure what it would include but hadn't realized that it would take so much of her life. But when she got the money and her dreams were secured, it would all be worth it. She could sacrifice a year of her life when it came to her future.

"And I want it to look, to everyone around us, like we are a real couple. That would involve going on dates, being romantic in public."

"Okay."

"I also think that at some point, you should move in with me."

"Move into your house?"

"It's what's best to maintain appearances."

Her throat had grown parched, so she desperately drank more milkshake. "And how long exactly do we have to be married?"

"Elias told me at least a year."

"So, this is actually a two-year commitment." Two years was a long time to pretend to be in love with another person. Especially with a man that she was attracted to… Especially with a man she'd slept with years ago, on a night that she still vividly remembered… Especially with a man who'd clearly said that this would strictly be a business arrangement.

"Yes. Are you still interested?" When she didn't answer right away, he put his elbows on the table and leaned closer. "You can back out," he told her. "But just remember. If you can't go along with this, let me know now, because getting control of the ranch is the most important thing to me."

A brief flash of unease tore through her. She'd promised herself that she would never again let herself be treated as second-class, and Garrett had made it known that Hardwell Ranch was his first priority.

"Willa?"

She realized that she hadn't said anything in a while. "I told you I would do it, and I'm a woman of my word."

"Thank you." He sat back and smiled. "So, we agree that this is a professional arrangement."

"Yeah, of course."

"I offered to pay you, and you declined. But now I have to insist. This is a business deal for both of us. That includes compensation."

Willa had been about to bring it up but was grateful that he had instead. "Yes."

A payday from Garrett would certainly fix most of her problems. She could pay off the debt and bills she'd amassed after the failed wedding and secure a loan to buy the property from Thomas.

"Name your price."

She'd expected him to offer her something, followed by a negotiation. But she had no idea where to start. "I have a figure in mind." She told him the amount of money she required to buy the property from Thomas, renovate it and open her inn. It was a substantial amount, but he didn't flinch.

"It's a deal."

"Just like that?" she asked, stunned by the casual way that wealthy people discussed money.

Garrett pushed aside his half-empty milkshake glass. "Well," he said, his voice holding more than a hint of innuendo, raising an eyebrow as he leaned across the table, "you're doing me this huge favor. Is there something else you want?"

She didn't miss his tone, and their eyes connected. There were things she wanted from him, but they suddenly had nothing to do with money. She forced herself to look away from him, and she thought about the things she could do with that money he'd offered. Of course, money wasn't everything, but she knew that with one check from Garrett, she could change her life.

She looked around the diner and saw that, even as she was thinking about it, people were staring, whispering to each other, and she knew exactly what they were talking about.

Even more than two years after the altar fiasco, she felt eyes on her everywhere she went in town. Their whispers trailed behind her, but she kept her head high, not showing any emotion. It wouldn't do any good to tell her side of the story—she'd tried to share her truth of what had happened behind the closed doors of her relationship with Thomas. The townspeople had already made up their minds. It was his story they believed. If marrying Garrett would take the focus off her past—that would be a nice benefit.

"It's not just the money," she told him. "I just want people to finally forget about me leaving my fiancé at the altar. If marrying you gives the residents of Applewood something else to discuss, then I'm all for it."

He nodded. "I can understand that."

The silence that hung between them was heavy, potent and in sharp contrast to the noise of chatting and clanging silverware against the dishes from the diner's other patrons. Willa wasn't sure how to fill the silence, but thankfully, the waitress appeared with their cheeseburgers.

"We'll discuss the rest of the payment details later," he said. "And I'll arrange a wire transfer for you once the ranch is signed over to me. But for now, you'll have to accept my undying love and appreciation for really helping me out of a bind."

She grinned and picked up her burger. "I'll take it." She raised her burger to her lips but stopped before taking a bite. "What about Dylan?" she asked him. There was no way her brother was going to be happy with them being in a relationship—fake or otherwise. And he was the excuse that Garrett had used years ago. "He loves you. But he's probably going to hate this."

Garrett didn't say anything for a moment. "I don't want to lie to him, but I can't tell him that we're faking a relationship. We can't tell anyone. I can't afford for it to get out."

"We can trust Dylan, though," Willa said. "He won't let it get back to Elias."

"I know that. But that's not everything. He looks up to Elias like he's his own grandfather. I can't ask him to lie to him to cover for me. It's best if he doesn't know it isn't real."

"You might be right," she said, unconvinced.

"But I still feel that we need to tell him at some point," she said. "I don't know how he would react. I need him and his support. I'm not like you. I don't come from a giant, loving family. Dylan and I had it pretty rough growing up, and he's all I have now."

Garrett sighed. "I'm embarrassed that I didn't think of it like that. I don't want to get between you and your brother." He rested his hand on top of hers. "We'll figure it out. Play it by ear. Will that put your mind at ease?"

"Okay. We'll figure it out together. But for now, let's put a pin in it. We can see how he reacts and go from there."

"Okay, that sounds good." Garrett nodded his head in the direction of the table of women, who were still covertly looking at them. "Let's give that table something to talk about and have a nice meal together."

She looked around the diner and noticed another group of women, whom they both had gone to school with, watching them intently. "Don't look now, but I feel like our charade is already starting to work."

Garrett conspiratorially looked at the women at the other table. He smiled at her and reached across the table and again placed his hand over hers. The way he rubbed his thumb over her knuckles, just his touch, his fingers over her skin—made her breath catch.

Garrett did something to her that no other man had managed to do. His presence affected Willa in such an acute way, and she was afraid that soon she would push their plates to the floor and jump across the table and kiss him. She pulled her hand back and fisted it into a ball in her lap. She forced herself to sit up straight and get a grip on her hormones and emotions—her head and her heart. She was only twenty minutes into the deal she'd made with Garrett. If the simple brush of his callused thumb over her knuckles was any indication, she was in for a long two years.

Four

Garrett's mind was on Willa as he walked into the kitchen of the main house. It was still early, coffee was on and Cathy had breakfast ready. Garrett mentally added finding a new cook and housekeeper for the main house to his mental list of things he'd need to do when Elias and Cathy moved on to their retirement life in Arizona. The house had been one of the fixtures of his childhood and into adulthood. He entered though the main door. The house was old, had been in the Hardwell family for generations; but while the fixtures had been updated—the finest money could buy—the wooden floors, scuffed as they were, had been maintained. Elias had always wanted it that way. The floors showed the life and history of the house, the old man had said. And Garrett agreed.

However, now there were moving boxes holding all of Cathy's and Elias's belongings. They'd begun packing their things, as part of their gradual move to Arizona. The thought of not having his grandfather around every day made Garrett sad. It was the end of an era of them working together. After Elias moved, the responsibility for the ranching business would solely fall on his shoulders. Provided he found a wife, of course. But he knew that that wouldn't be a problem for him. He had Willa.

He walked into the expansive, bright, fully renovated kitchen. The appliances were almost industrial sized, to accommodate food for meals for the ranch's entire staff. For the most part, the ranch hands worked together, lived together and ate together. They were as much family as blood relatives, and that was what made them such a good and successful loyal team.

From the kitchen, he looked into the dining room. Several ranch hands were already seated at the large oak table by the window—the same table that had sat in the main house kitchen since Elias's own grandparents owned the property. Every morning, Cathy made a huge, diverse spread, which included fruit, and a hearty mixture of eggs, oatmeal and assorted breakfast meats.

Morning was always a calm time for everyone on the ranch, when they were all allowed a moment to contemplate the day ahead and the work that would need to be done as they filled up on eggs and bacon.

Garrett greeted them all and poured himself a coffee. He was just bringing the mug to his lips when Dylan walked in. He grabbed a mug from the cupboard, and Garrett, who was still holding the carafe, poured him a mug of coffee. He thought about how Dylan would respond to his dating Willa—real or otherwise.

"Can I talk to you outside for a bit?"

He lowered his mug. "Can't wait until I finish my coffee?"

"Afraid not." He turned and walked out to the front porch, and Dylan followed. Garrett had been thinking about how he was going to tell Dylan about his relationship with Willa. Would he tell him the truth, keep up the lie? He would have to see how Dylan reacted before deciding. When they were alone outside, they drank from their mugs for several moments, until Dylan finally spoke.

"So, what's up?"

"I've been thinking about something, and I wanted to run it by you before I did it."

"I can't imagine why you'd need my approval to do anything."

"I might for this. I want to ask Willa to be my date to the fundraising gala tomorrow night."

Dylan was raising his mug to his lips, but he paused halfway as Garrett stopped and looked at him. "What? Why?"

"I don't have a date," he said simply. "I thought she might like to join me."

"As a casual, friend-like thing?"

Here was the sticky part. Garrett could easily tell Dylan that he and Willa had formed an agreement to fake date and get married, but Dylan went so far back with Elias, and his grandfather had helped Dylan more than either of them could say. Garrett didn't want to put his friend in a position to have to lie to Elias. Plus, the fewer people who knew about their secret, the better. So, Garrett made the decision to lie. It wouldn't be the first time he'd lie about whatever interest he had in Willa. He'd managed to keep the night they'd slept together a secret from his friend, he could do it again, and there was nothing stopping he and Willa from telling him the truth later if they had to.

"Not necessarily," he clarified, knowing that this could easily go sideways. Dylan could be pissed to hear that he was interested in his younger sister.

"Where's this coming from?"

"We ran into each other briefly at the engagement party. We used to be closer back in the day, and I'd like to get to know her a bit better."

Garrett wasn't sure how to read his friend's impassive face. "You know everything she's been through in the past two years, right?"

"I know some of it. You know I don't listen to gossip."

Dylan shook his head. "I'd hate to see her get hurt again."

"I'm not going to hurt her."

"I know. But I need you to know that I won't sit by and watch her get jerked around."

That offended Garrett. Dylan was his friend, was that what he thought about her? "What the hell, man? If that's what you think I do—"

"Hold up," Dylan said, shutting him up. "Listen, you're my best friend, and I know more about you than God himself. I also know that you've hooked up with your share of women."

"Right." Garrett couldn't deny either of those facts. As a younger man, any time not spent on the ranch, he'd spent chasing women. "But you know I've changed."

"If you promise to do right by my sister, I'll approve."

Garrett smiled. "Thanks."

"But don't think I won't kick your ass six ways from Sunday if you do anything to mess with her."

"Cross my heart, man."

"Good."

The sun was getting higher in the sky, and though Garrett was happy that Dylan had had a positive reaction, he wanted to get the topic of discussion off his personal life and Willa. "What are you doing today?"

Dylan put down his coffee cup and stood. "I'm going to head out to the southern boundary of the ranch. One of the hands discovered last night that the fence needs some mending."

Garrett hadn't heard about that, and he hated being kept out of the loop when it came to things on the ranch. It felt like the more he became involved in the business side of ranching, taking over things Elias normally dealt with, and working on the transition of management and ownership, the harder it was for him to stay connected to the land. That's why he had Dylan. "No one told me about that."

Dylan shrugged. "It's not a big deal. I don't believe the break is big enough for anything to get in or out. I put some patrols out that way last night to check on predators or any cows displaced from the herd, and the cameras haven't captured anything out of the ordinary either. It was secured last night, and now we're going to fix it permanently."

"That's good. Get someone to take a ride and check the rest of the perimeter. Make sure there aren't any other weaknesses."

"Already taken care of," Dylan assured him. "Nico is going to do a run along it today."

"Thanks for being on top of it. Want me to come with?"

Dylan shook his head. "No. I'm good. We've got it under control." For the first time that Garrett could remember, there was an awkward silence between him and his friend, and he worried that the deal with Willa was already started to affect their relationship. Dylan spoke first and stretched his arms over his head. "But I should get out to the southern fence. The guys are probably already out there."

Alone on the porch, Garrett thought about the upcoming weeks, months, years. He was about to start dating Willa—no, *fake dating*—in order to get what

he wanted. But that also meant he would have to re-
move himself from the way he felt about her. Every
time she was near, his body reacted. He wanted to
get close to her, closer than he was. But this was
certainly a harebrained way to go about it. He had
to keep his eyes on the prize. He looked around the
ranch—that was the prize. He had to forget his li-
bido and focus on making sure Hardwell Ranch came
under his power.

He watched Dylan, now on his horse, as he headed
for the southern boundary. Keeping the fake relationship between him and Willa was the safest thing for
their arrangement. At least his friend had seemed
okay with the idea of him asking Willa out. At least,
that's how it seemed. There was no telling what was
going on in Dylan's mind, but Garrett felt bad for
not telling him the whole truth. "Worry 'bout that
later," he muttered to himself, as he walked back
into the house.

Willa left the main house of Hardwell Ranch with
a smile on her face. She'd had another successful
meeting with Cathy, during which they'd gone over
the woman's preferred wedding invitations. The
whole time, however, Willa was on edge, alternately
hoping she would and wouldn't see Garrett coming
around a corner or into the main house. At the back
of her mind, she wondered if she should go find him.
If they were going to fake a relationship, would it
seem strange that she didn't go look for him? She had

no idea how to play a fake relationship. She would have to just follow his lead.

Luckily, she didn't have to wonder for long, because he was on the front porch when she opened the door and slammed straight into the hard warmth of his chest.

"Oh!" she said, the force and surprise knocking the air from her lungs. She looked up and saw the good humor in his smile. "Hi," she said.

"Hello, darlin'," he said with the sexiest drawl she could have imagined. "We've got to stop meeting like this. I didn't expect to see you here today. It's a nice surprise."

"I was meeting with Cathy."

"You have an awful lot of meetings with her."

"Well, of course. I'm her wedding coordinator," she explained. "And she has some very specific ideas about what she's looking for. She likes to make sure that we're in close communication every day."

"Are you sure you aren't looking for reasons to run into me?"

"Aren't you full of yourself?"

"No, I just know that you can't stay away from me," he teased. "But either way, this is my good luck. If I didn't have a few meetings this afternoon, I'd suggest we get lunch."

She held up her hands. "I can't do any more than one of Patsy's cheeseburgers in a week. Plus, I'm busy today."

"Either way, I'm glad I ran into you." He paused. "I talked to Dylan."

"And?"

"I told him that I wanted to take you to Daisy's fundraising gala."

"Oh, did you now?"

"I told him I was interested in getting to know you better."

"Good start. And what did he say?"

"In no uncertain terms, he would kick my ass if I wronged you."

"That sounds about right," she said with a laugh, knowing how protective her brother was.

"So what do you say?" he asked her. "Do you have plans tomorrow night?"

She shook her head. "I don't."

"How would you like to join me at the vet-clinic fundraising gala?"

The town vet, Daisy, was one of her closest friends. She'd known about the fundraiser and had contributed financially, of course, but she'd had no plans of purchasing a table (no single tickets available) to the gala that had been organized by the Applewood Hospitality Group—which mostly consisted of some of the town's rich housewives, the ladies who lunched, who had nothing better to do than sip pinot grigio while they planned events to further their own status in town and gossip about others. She would much rather stay home and curl up on the couch with a book. "I don't know," she told him.

"Come on," he prodded. "I've got a table. It'd be a good time to show the world that we're now a couple.

We can set a little of that good fake-dating ground-work."

He was right. They needed to get on with the actual "relationship" part of their fake relationship. This would be the first test for them. It would be their first date at a formal social event together—their coming out, one could say. She also knew that, because it was a fundraiser, it would be attended by all of Applewood's most elite citizens, and the people there would likely have something to say to her—whether to her face or behind her back... Behind the back was more Applewood's style. It wasn't something she was looking forward to. "You have a table? Who else is going to be there?"

"Just some friends and family members. My father and stepmother, Cathy, Elias—I also invited Dylan. All friendly faces. You know, nothing too scary."

Nothing too scary. That's what Garrett thought. He didn't know just how vicious and hurtful some of the townspeople could be. He didn't know what they were capable of. That was bad, but also, when she'd said goodbye to Thomas, she'd also said goodbye to the designer clothing and accessories, the monthly salon visits. She mentally scanned through her closet in her apartment in High Pine, which ran a range from business casual to her favorite T-shirts and yoga pants. "I don't exactly have anything to wear to a gala," she said.

"Don't worry about it for a second," he said. "I asked Cathy, and she gave me some recommendations. I've got a designer coming in from Austin, and he'll have a few things you can try on. I'll pass on his number, and you can send him your size and the styles you like. And I've also arranged something called a 'glam squad' for you."

She was impressed by his desire to accommodate her. "That's mighty presumptuous of you, assuming that you'd just tell me you wanted me to come to the gala with you, and I'd jump at it."

He shrugged. "It's a good meal, at a popular event, for a good cause. Plus, I figured since you haven't lived here in a while, it would be an excellent time for you to network with some folks around here. That's what your business hinges on, right?"

It was true. She could network a little and find some clients looking to plan different kinds of events. She could even look into planning fundraising events. But she didn't know how many people would be interested in talking to her. Maybe it wouldn't hurt to meet some new people, if they weren't part of the gossipy cliques. But as long as she was taking her life back, it was time for her to face her challenges. And tomorrow night, one of those challenges would be the people of Applewood.

"Yeah, I'd love to go with you."

Garrett smiled. "Great. Why don't you come here after work tomorrow, and we'll get you all set up?"

"Would it be all right if we meet at Dylan's? I'll be coming from work, and his place is closer to High Pine." She'd agreed to the arrangement with Garrett, but part of her was wary to give up every bit of control to him. This wouldn't be a one-sided deal, where she lost her autonomy and just went along with what he wanted.

Garrett's gaze wavered briefly, as if taken aback by her change in his plans. "Yeah, that's fine," he said after a moment. "I'll just get everyone to go to his place instead." They were quiet for several beats, and he looked off into the distance where a couple of ranch hands were hauling bales of hay. "I've got to get back to work."

"Yeah, me too." She had meetings lined up in High Pine for the afternoon. More weddings. Soon, she'd be planning a wedding of her own.

She watched Garrett walk away, and the way that his Levi's clung to his backside, and her thoughts drifted to what it would be like to be married to him. A warmth that had nothing to do with the summer sun flushed her cheeks, and she forced herself to look away from him. She clenched her fists and walked back to her car, not allowing herself to look back at him. "This is a business relationship," she reminded herself. "Not a romantic one." Garrett knew that... why didn't she?

Five

The next day, Willa left work early. She had to get ready for the gala she didn't want to attend, and she knew that first she needed a run first to clear her head. Her exercise regimen had been recently interrupted due to work, so she tried to get a run in whenever she could.

She drove to Dylan's house and, using the key he'd given her, let herself in through the back door. Dylan had bought the place for cheap after he'd started to do well at the ranch., and she'd lived with him there until she'd moved in with Thomas. The house had been in hard shape, but they'd both worked together to fix the place up. It was the first time since they were very young and had lost their parents in car accident, that they'd ever felt like they had a home.

She brought her bag to the room she had claimed as her own. Just having a bedroom there reminded her that even though she'd had a rough upbringing, Applewood was home, and before the whole Thomas debacle, she'd been happy enough there. Changing out of her work clothes, she pulled on her workout gear. She put her buds in her ears, ran down the porch stairs and jogged to the road. She didn't have a particular path in mind for her run, but Willa knew where she would end up.

She ran down Applewood's Main Street, past all the quaint shops that had stood the test of time, and the new brewpubs and cafés that stood alongside the century-old post office, city hall and fire hall. She kept her head up and looked past the townspeople lunching at outdoor tables. Surprisingly, for the first time in a long time, she found herself not caring as much what they may be thinking of her. She moved past them.

Willa's heart was pounding as she took the quiet, less-traveled dirt road that would take her to the property she visited every time she was in Applewood. A few years ago, through some research, she'd discovered that the one-hundred-and-fifty-year-old home had originally belonged to her family. As a girl who'd grown up without her parents, or any other family, she'd felt a connection to her roots through the property, and she'd wanted to buy it, even if she hadn't the means.

Willa glared at the For Sale sign that was posted on the overgrown lawn. Her mistake had been revealing to her former fiancé, Thomas, that her future dreams hung on buying the mansion, renovating it and opening an inn. But after their ill-fated wedding, in a move of revenge, he'd outright bought the place, and knowing what it meant to her, told her that he would gladly sell it back to her—for twice its original price. There were no other interested buyers, so the property was still on the market, waiting for her. He would just as soon let the place rot before he let her have it without paying an exorbitant amount of money to him.

She looked up at the building and pictured it in all of its restored glory. Just looking at the place filled her with hope for her future—she could stop working for someone else, working at a job that she didn't want to do, and become her own boss; she could use the hospitality and business management degree she'd earned in college—and with the payout from Garrett, she might be able to actually pay what Thomas wanted.

Her cell phone—which was strapped to her biceps, playing her running playlist—vibrated, and the music in her earbuds stopped playing. She was getting a phone call. She answered without checking the caller ID. "Hi, this is Willa," she said, hoping that her heavy breathing wasn't evident on the other end.

"Will," Dylan said. "Where are you?"

"I went for a run. What's up?"

"Do you know anything about a designer and some other people coming here for you?"

She'd spent too long daydreaming and her run had

gone on so long. "Oh yeah, I thought Garrett might have told you about that."

"He sure didn't."

"Okay, well, I'll be right back. Just invite them in."

"Of course, I did—did you think I just left them outside?"

"Be right there."

When Willa arrived at Dylan's home, she hadn't expected the place to have been transformed into a fashion boutique. She looked around the living room. Kristoph, the designer Garrett had contacted, had brought two racks of dresses in her size.

"Hi. Sorry I'm late," she told Kristoph. "I didn't realize you'd be here yet."

He ignored her apology, and looked her up and down, taking in her sweaty running wear, wild hair and flushed face. "Well, I knew I was here to dress some rich man's girlfriend, but I didn't realize we were going to need a full-on Cinderella makeover here." Willa opened her mouth, ready to be offended, but Kristoph laughed. "Sweety, I'm just kidding. You're already too gorgeous for words. You just go shower and we'll finish setting up here."

"Okay, thanks?" she said, almost too bewildered to respond.

Twenty minutes later, fresh from her shower and wearing a silky robe that Kristoph had brought for her, she browsed through the selection of formal dresses. She couldn't believe that Garrett had such a service at his disposal—to just pay a well-known designer to drive in from Austin to loan her a gown. After trying on what felt like two dozen dresses, they settled on a full-length emerald green gown that had a slit up to her thigh and fit like it was made just for her.

After they'd settled that matter, the "glam squad" Garrett had mentioned arrived, complete with a hair stylist, makeup artist and a manicurist.

The way they bustled around her as they got set up, she felt like an overwhelmed princess-to-be getting ready for the ball. Maybe Kristoph hadn't been wrong about the Cinderella comparison. She was guided—more so pulled—to a chair in front of a brightly lit mirror. It was too much, the attention they all paid: moving around her; testing shades; framing her face with their hands; pulling her hair back, up, to the side.

Soon, they all got down to work, somehow in tandem. The manicurist polished her nails as the stylist worked wonders with her hair, giving her a blowout. The sheer volume of her hair surprised her. "You know, this style is a bit bigger than I normally go with," she told the aptly named stylist, Blade.

Blade smiled at her in the mirror. "Well, you know how it goes in Texas, honey," he cracked. "The higher the hair…"

He didn't need to the finish the line. Willa laughed and took in her reflection. Her hair was more glamorous than she'd ever worn it. Without her staple ponytail or French twist, she was already nearly unrecognizable. The makeup artist then swiftly moved in and began applying foundation. She had never before in her life felt so pampered. Not even when she'd been with Thomas had he ever treated her to such a spectacle. She frowned. After she'd left him, she'd built herself a quiet, simple life. This was something she wasn't used to anymore. Willa couldn't help but draw comparisons between the men. Sure, Garrett was a gentleman, he was kind, sexy, funny—everything that Thomas wasn't—but when she thought of the money that Garrett had, her stomach twisted as it triggered something unpleasant within her. The pampering, the opulence, brought back painful memories of the last wealthy man she'd planned to marry.

She should be grateful—and she was—but it was difficult to picture her life for the next couple of years as Garrett's girlfriend/fiancée/wife if this were to become the norm. Would she transform into the quiet but elegant woman that Thomas had wanted her to be? Would playing Garrett's doting wife leave her forgetting her struggles and the person she'd grown into?

"How do you feel about this lipstick?" the makeup artist asked, interrupting her thoughts, holding a tube of red color that she'd have never selected for herself. It was a deep shade that would make her stand out among the other partygoers. A meeker version of Willa surely would not wear such a color. She wouldn't fade into the crowd this time. "I love it. Let's use it."

* * *

The limo drove up Dylan's driveway. Garrett got out and climbed the stairs, rolling his shoulders against the confines of his black suit. He hated dressing up in formal wear as much as he hated the galas and balls that required them. If the evening's party hadn't been a fundraiser for Daisy and her vet clinic, he would be home on the couch with an ice-cold beer.

He straightened his jacket and knocked on the door. Dylan answered, also in a black suit and looking just as miserable.

"Hey," he said.

"Hi," Dylan responded. "That might be the first time you've knocked on the door to this house. Or are you just trying to be respectful because you're here to pick up my sister for a date?" he asked with a frown. Garrett said nothing, unsure how to proceed, wondering why exactly he had knocked. He regretted it, fearing he'd made things awkward with his friend, but Dylan cracked a smile. "I'm kidding. Come on in. Want a beer?" Dylan asked.

"Yeah, sure."

Dylan pulled a couple of bottles from the fridge, opened both and handed one to Garrett.

"Thanks," he said before both men raised the frosty bottles to their lips. The beer was cold and quenched his thirst.

"I assume you're to blame for the beauty salon in my living room this afternoon?"

"Sorry about that. I wanted to make sure she had

everything she needed for tonight. She suggested doing it here. I probably should have told you."

"Not a problem." He looked down at his fingers. "They buffed my nails real nice. And told me I ought to be using more moisturizer."

Garrett looked at his friend's tanned hands. His fingernails were indeed shiny and manicured—a stark contrast to the nicks and calluses that came with working on the ranch. "Looks good."

"Don't knock it until you try it."

"Well, let's skip the football game next weekend and get manicures."

They laughed together, and Garrett was relieved. He'd been worried at first that Dylan wouldn't be happy about him dating Willa, but so far, he seemed okay with it.

"Nice ride," Dylan said, nodding in the direction of the black limo.

Garrett grinned, a bit embarrassed by the opulence. He shouldn't have gone so "extra" with their transportation. "I figured 'why not?' I need to look the part of the ranch owner. Might as well go in style."

"Nothing wrong with that."

"You're riding with us, right?"

Dylan shrugged. "I was just going to take my truck."

"Don't worry about it. There's more than enough room," he said, trying to make amends with his friend even in this small way.

"I guess I might as well. Thanks."

Garrett looked around. "Is Willa ready?"

"Pretty much. She's upstairs."

A silence fell over them as they drank their beer, until they heard a noise coming from the staircase.

Garrett looked up and saw that Willa was ready. Too bad he wasn't, because he almost choked on his beer. He swallowed roughly, but he still found himself unable to speak. The only word he could muster was a surprised "Wow."

Willa smiled and descended the stairs. She was wearing a long green dress that fit her perfectly, and as far as he could tell, her hair and makeup were flawless. But it was her smile that about did him in. Willa, so normally reserved, considered prickly by many, smiled brightly, seeming to luxuriate in her makeover.

"You look beautiful," he told her, and forgetting about Dylan's existence, he took several steps to stand in front of her.

"Thank you. Although, I should probably be thanking you for arranging this. I can't remember the last time I was pampered like that."

"You deserve it."

"You like the dress?" she asked, doing a little spin. Garrett couldn't take his eyes off her generous curves under that green silk, and his body tensed with desire. He didn't know seeing her this way would affect him so much.

"It's like it was made for you."

"I'm glad you like it."

Garrett heard Dylan clear his throat behind them, the noise startling him. He didn't want to admit that he'd all but forgotten Dylan was still in the room. "I don't want to interrupt anything," Dylan said. "But we should probably get going."

In the back of the limo, Willa sat beside Garrett, while Dylan sat on the seat that was perpendicular to them. The inside was quiet, and she hoped that the awkwardness wouldn't last between them. She'd heard the two men talking and laughing while they waited downstairs, and she was relieved that Dylan wasn't upset that she and Garrett were attending the event together. But his silence made her question how he really felt about the budding relationship.

Although, his just being there seemed like a good sign.

"I hate these parties," Dylan muttered.

"Just think of it as an opportunity to hit on women and take advantage of the open bar," Garrett supplied.

"Just like the good old days," Dylan agreed.

"Yeah, the good ol' days," Willa added, rolling her eyes. "I can't believe I'm about to go to another Applewood gala. I certainly thought those days were behind me." She'd attended similar events and functions on Thomas's arm many times. As long as she'd known her place and played her part as the cordial and polite politician's fiancée, she had fit right in with that crowd. She sighed. She couldn't believe that she was about to go into the lioness's den again.

The car stopped, and the driver opened the door closest to Garrett. He exited and held his hand to escort Willa out. She took his hand and pivoted her body, sliding gracefully from the car. Dylan followed behind. There were several photographers from the *Applewood Tribune*, the town's small paper, which took itself far too seriously with its honest-to-goodness High Society page. People paused in front of the step-and-repeat banner that had been created for the event, par for the course for Applewood's ruling class. She watched as people took their place and smiled for the camera. She would have said something snide, but she stopped herself, remembering these people were all there to raise money for her friend Daisy's veterinary clinic.

Dylan went on ahead, skipping the photography and heading straight for the door and the open bar inside. As their turn neared on the photo line, Garrett must have sensed her hesitation. "You sure you still want to do this?" Garrett asked, sliding his arm low around her waist, pulling her close. She could feel the way his work-roughened hands caught in the silk, and she imagined the way his fingers would feel on her skin.

Willa exhaled and nodded. But she didn't like being escorted into the fundraising gala like a kept woman. That was something she'd hated from her previous life, and she never wanted to be that again. Willa always wanted to keep her head up high. But it was difficult, especially knowing who would be inside. Her former friends, the family that was almost hers.

Her former fiancé.

"Are you okay?"

Willa realized that she hadn't responded to his first question. She looked up at him. "Yeah, I'm fine."

"You know, we don't have to go in. We can just get back in the car and go."

"No," she said firmly. "We are going in there. We need to do this. It's our first event as a couple." Knowing that people had already noticed them there together, with his arm still around her waist, she turned to face him. In a move that made them look like a loving couple, she placed her two palms on his chest as the photographer snapped their photo. She smiled at Garrett, looking up at him as a doting girlfriend would. "We're going to go right in there. We're going to have dinner. We'll dance, convince everyone that we're together and then you're going to write Daisy a big fat check for the clinic."

He smiled. "Well, I was planning on doing all of that anyway," he assured her. And before she had a chance to move, he lowered his head and put his lips on hers. She felt the breath leave her lungs as he kissed her, and she was only partly aware of the gasps and murmurs from those around them. Just as quickly as the kiss had begun, it ended, and he pulled away. "But if you're ready, let's go."

With his arm still around her waist, he ushered her inside, secure in the knowledge that their picture would, no doubt, show up in the paper. That would lend credence to their charade and help Elias believe they were in a relationship, but on the flip side of that, it would leave people talking about whether or not the "runaway bride" and the town's most eligible bachelor were an item. She looked over at Garrett. He was a rugged man, a rancher who worked hard, and he looked good in his typical uniform of Levi's and boots; but in his impeccably fitted black suit and cowboy hat, he looked every bit as sexy.

They walked inside, and Willa wasn't surprised by the gazes that were cast in their direction. News that they were there together had spread over the last two minutes. Garrett seemed oblivious to it, however, as he led her to the bar. She was grateful; a drink would help relax her enough to get through the evening. It could have been her imagination, but as they walked through the room, like in a movie, the crowd seemed to part in front of them, as if to make way for them. But as they progressed, she could then feel their eyes on her back, watching her as they navigated the crowd of Applewood's elite residents.

It felt like a lifetime ago, but she had once mixed in this circle. She may have been engaged to Thomas, Applewood's mayor, but she'd felt that she didn't belong. As a child, she'd always been considered the girl from the other side of the tracks. She'd been as surprised as everyone else when Thomas saw her working at Patsy's one fateful night and took an interest in her. However, with their snide remarks and sideways glances, the top tier of Applewood's social structure had never let her forget where she'd come from. And from the looks of things now, they still hadn't.

Despite the odds, though, Thomas had chosen her. She didn't understand how she'd been so lucky. At first. He'd won her over with his words, the attention he lavished on her—the vacations, the parties, they were just an added bonus. Especially for a foster girl from the other side of town. But soon, things had changed. She hadn't noticed it at first. But he'd tried to change her. He wanted influence over what she wore, what she did, who she was. It had been a subtle shift, but over time, she had almost lost everything she was.

What she didn't know was why it took her so long to realize what she had given up—maybe it was the text messages and pictures of another woman that she'd seen on his phone, just seconds before she was due to walk down the aisle, that sent her over the edge. She hadn't even had a moment to process her decision before the music had started and it was time to meet him at the altar and give him the rest of her life. Gripping her bouquet in sweaty palms and marching down to the beat of her pounding heart, she saw her husband-to-be, and something inside her snapped. *I'm not doing this*, she'd said before dropping her bouquet at his feet and running back the way she'd entered.

She'd always been an outsider to them, but since that day, she'd been persona non grata in Applewood society. She'd lost a lot of her business contacts and people she'd thought were friends. These same people were now watching her with a look of confusion, mixed with equal parts interest and disdain.

So, she kept her head straight and focused on a spot on the wall behind the bar in an attempt to tune out everything else.

"I can't believe she's here."

"With Garrett Hardwell."

"He's got a lot of money headed his way once Elias retires."

"She just wants a piece of it."

She hated that people still had these feelings about her. But she had to ignore it. She knew the truth. They didn't. They didn't know the terrible way Thomas had treated her. According to Applewood's citizens, he was still the upstanding citizen he always had been.

Garrett handed her a glass of wine, which pulled her from her trip down memory lane. "How do you feel?"

She nodded. "Fine." She didn't have high hopes for the evening, but she knew she would get through it. She'd lived through worse. A few whispers and glares weren't going to deter her from her goal of marrying Garrett and getting her life back. She sipped her drink and heard more conversation behind her.

"I hope she doesn't do to Garrett what she did to Thomas."

"Gold digger."

She drank down the wine and put the empty glass down on the bar. "Want another?" Garrett asked, an eyebrow raised.

"I probably shouldn't," she told him, feeling the

warmth of the wine in her stomach and radiating through her veins.

They turned away from the bar, and then she saw him. Thomas was standing near the podium at the front of the room, regaling some hangers-on and making them laugh out loud in that phony way, commanding the attention of everyone in the room.

She stilled. It was the first time she'd laid eyes on her former fiancé since she'd left town. She turned to Garrett, who was seemingly oblivious to Thomas's presence on the other side of the room.

"Thomas is over there," she said quietly to Garrett.

Garrett looked in the man's direction without staring. "Screw him. Ignore him. I'm here with you."

"I know. But I can hear people talking about me." She hated that it still bothered her so much. She'd learned to become secure in who she was, but all it took was five minutes around these people to bring all the self-doubt back.

"Forget about them," he told her. "Forget about Thomas and all of the gossipy old biddies." She smiled, and he took her hand and drew her to the hardwood dance floor. "Let's dance."

He grasped her hand with one of his, while his other hand rested low on her back, pressing against her as he pulled her close—probably closer than he needed to, but she didn't mind. She felt stiff at first, knowing that people were watching them and wondering out loud what Garrett Hardwell was doing with a woman like Willa; but when she looked up at

Garrett, his green eyes were only on her. She relaxed, and she could feel her body loosen, taking pleasure in the heat from his firm chest and strong arms, as he led her through the dance.

The rich, soulful voice of Charley Pride filled the room and more people joined them on the dance floor. Willa sang along and felt Garrett's eyes on her and she looked at him, embarrassed. "Sorry," he said.

"It's okay. There's nothing like that old country, right? It really brings you back in time."

He nodded and pulled her closer. "You're so right."

"You're a good dancer."

He chuckled, and she could feel the vibration from his chest. "I've got talents you know nothing about," he told her.

She nestled closer. "I'm sure you do."

He pulled her even closer, and together they swayed to the music. The room fell away, and soon she forgot about everyone else and their opinions. There was only Garrett. The print of his lips was burned onto hers. She had been shocked by the kiss at first, but like this dance, she had fallen into it, melted against him.

"Sorry I didn't give you any warning about that— the kiss," he murmured, somehow reading her mind. "It felt like the right thing to do at the time. Every- one was watching."

Willa straightened, reminded that this was an ar- rangement, not a relationship. He'd kissed her be- cause of their charade, not because he was overtaken by romantic desire for her. She felt like a fool, being so easily swept away, picturing happily-ever-afters because of his touch. "It was fine," she said. "It was a good show. It definitely got people talking."

When the song ended, Willa stepped away from him. "I'm going to head to the ladies' room."

Garrett grinned. "Time to powder your nose?"

"Yeah. Something like that," she said, not looking at him. Tension had taken up residence in her body, replacing the languid comfort she'd previously felt in his arms.

He must have sensed her change in demeanor. "Everything okay?"

"Yeah, it's fine," she told him, but the narrowing of his eyes told her that he didn't quite believe her. She walked away from him before he could say anything else.

Willa had hoped she could be alone in the bathroom, and when she heard the water running in the sink, she cringed, and almost turned on her heel to leave.

"What are you doing here?" the woman said behind her.

Willa turned to see Daisy, one of her best friends, and the town vet whose clinic was benefiting from the gala. She reached out for Willa, and they embraced. "Thank God you're here," Daisy said. "I appreciate the help for the clinic, but these things are so boring."

"You're telling me. I had to come in here and hide."

"You might be the last person I expected to see here tonight."

"I didn't really expect to be here."

Daisy put her hands on Willa's shoulders and held her at arm's length, taking in her makeover. "And look at this dress. What is going on?"

Willa explained how Garrett had asked her to attend the gala, leaving out, however, the whole fake-marriage-for-an-inheritance thing. If they hadn't yet told Dylan the whole thing was a charade, she didn't think it was fair to tell anyone else.

Daisy's eyes widened. "Impressive. Garrett's a good one. I'm glad you're getting back out there."

"I'm not getting out anywhere," Willa insisted. "He's an old friend."

"I'll bet."

"You don't look as convinced as everyone else out there."

Daisy frowned. "Anyone giving you a hard time?"

"Just some comments that I'm trying to ignore."

"Good for you. You're here in a gorgeous dress with a smoking hot dude. Forget about them."

"As far as advice goes, that's not bad."

Daisy leaned against the wall. "So, about Garrett, when did that start, exactly? Is there anything going on between the two of you?"

"No," she told her friend. "We saw each other at his grandfather's engagement party a couple of nights ago."

"Oh, right. The old man is finally remarrying,"

she said with a chuckle. "How was the party? Perfect, I assume, because you planned it."

"Why weren't you there?" she asked. "I know you were invited."

"I had an out-of-town appointment that day and didn't get back until late."

"I guess you didn't hear what happened then." She shook her head. Daisy was never one to gossip and for that Willa was grateful. She told her about Elias's requirement that Garrett settle down and find a wife.

"Garrett Hardwell has to get married," Daisy said with a laugh. "That should be fun to see. Although there's certainly no shortage of women around here who wouldn't mind being the wife of a wealthy rancher."

Willa laughed but didn't tell her friend that they had already agreed on getting married. Again, she found herself lying to someone she loved. If she couldn't get through a night of lying to her brother or best friend, this would be a tough couple of years. It would be a lot easier to tell them both the truth, but Garrett wanted to keep it their secret, and she had to respect that. "Yeah, really."

"In fact, you'd better watch out. You might be the one he asks."

"I don't think so. I'm never putting myself through anything like a marriage again."

"Not even for a guy like Garrett? He was always a nice guy. I think you guys would be really compatible."

"He is a nice guy." But not only that, they had

real chemistry. Nobody—not even Daisy—knew about the one night she'd spent in Garrett's arms. She already knew that they were compatible in almost every way.

Garrett sipped his beer as he stood within view of the bathroom door. He frowned behind his glass. He knew that something had upset Willa, and he looked around at everyone who had no doubt been talking about her. He hated that she was upset. He wanted to go in there and get her, to bring her home—away from everyone who'd made her feel like a lesser person.

He remembered how it had felt to have his hands on her, sliding over the silk of her dress, the one that fit her like a second skin. He remembered the way that the heat from her body permeated his clothing, and he imagined how her bare skin would feel under his fingertips. He let his mind wander, and he imagined them moving together, skin-to-skin, their beating hearts pounding against each other, their mouths joining as he slid—Garrett blinked the image away when he saw Thomas walking toward him, taking long, confident strides across the ballroom. He gulped down his beer to lower his body temperature and adjusted his jacket over his midsection so no one would be any the wiser about his innermost thoughts and fantasies.

"Hardwell," Thomas said when he was close enough.

"Thomas."

"I see you're here with Willa Statler tonight."

"That's right. I am."

"I'm just going to warn you right now. Be careful of that one."

Garrett bristled. He'd known Willa for years. He trusted her and didn't need to be careful of anything when it came to her. "Don't worry about me."

"I'm serious. She tried to extort me for a payout after the biggest humiliation of my life. Walked out on our wedding—I'm sure you've heard about that."

"What extortion?" He'd heard the rumors about Willa. She'd told him herself that Thomas had left her with debts, and she'd needed to start a new life.

"She left me at the altar and then tried to take me for almost six figures."

Garrett knew that he probably shouldn't take Thomas's word as gospel, but he wanted to know what had happened. He knew that she'd left her former fiancé at the altar, but he hadn't known anything about her demands for money. He didn't believe the man, but he wanted more information. "Is that right?"

"It is," he warned. "I know you're looking to take over Hardwell Ranch. I've done a lot of business with your grandfather, and he's an important man in town."

"What's my grandfather have to do with this?"

"Hardwell Ranch might be successful around the world. But I would hate to see all of his hard work and the goodwill that he's earned in this town go to waste."

Garrett laughed. "No other ranch in this area

has the distribution deals that we do. And that's not even to discuss our reputation in raising and training horses. Your threats don't mean a damn to me."

He could see the red raise in Thomas's cheeks. "You know as well as I do that no matter the success you have, the ranching world is small, and the opinions of the citizens of Applewood have a significant impact on your reputation." Garrett knew that was somewhat true; Applewood was home to many influential people. But he chose not to say anything. "Willa's not wanted in these circles," Thomas continued. "She's burned her bridges. I'd hate for you to be caught in the cross fire."

Still, Garrett was undeterred. "Is it that Willa is not wanted in these circles? Or is it that you and your ilk don't want her here because she didn't give you what you wanted?"

Thomas glowered and puffed out his chest in a move Garrett knew he used to intimidate others. It didn't work on Garrett, though. "Just be careful of that one."

"Don't worry about me."

The bathroom door opened, and Willa, along with Daisy, stepped out just as Thomas walked away. She watched with a notable scowl as he disappeared into the crowd. "What did he want?"

Garrett shook his head, not wanting to burden Willa with what Thomas had said about her. "Nothing. He was just saying hello."

Willa narrowed her eyes. She obviously didn't believe him. She watched him closely, waiting for him to say more—but he didn't. Thankfully, she dropped it. "All right, fine."

"Should we head to our table?" he asked. "I believe dinner will be served soon."

She took the offer, looping her hand around his biceps. "Yes, let's," she said, smiling. He noted that it didn't quite reach her eyes.

As they found their seats, Garrett's family greeted them. Even if the rest of the people at the party were cold to her, at least he could count on his loved ones to treat her with respect. They weren't gossips and didn't listen to tall tales that spread through the town like wildfire. She fit right in with his family, and they accepted her. He knew he could count on his original feelings about her. He'd considered her a friend, but the stirring in his gut made him wonder if he wanted more.

The night drew to a close, and people started to leave. Garrett's table was now empty, save for them. He looked over and caught Willa's small, polite yawn.

"Are you ready to leave?" he asked her.

"Yeah, I definitely am."

Garrett stood and pulled back Willa's chair as she got up from the table. When she stood, he took yet another moment to check out how her impeccable body looked in her formfitting dress. "You know, I'm going to have to buy that dress for you. I can't imagine anyone looking as good as you do in it."

She smiled. "You're just saying that because I'm your fake girlfriend."

"You're right. But I'm also saying it because it's true."

Garrett put his hand on Willa's lower waist, feeling the frisson of energy that traveled between them at the slightest touch. She must have felt it, too, because she looked up at him, her eyes wide and lips slightly parted. He thought of the way he'd kissed her outside. He'd lied to her, of course. He'd told her that he'd done it for the benefit of those who'd been watching. But that hadn't been it. He'd all but forgotten about everything when he looked down at her then. She'd been so stunning, so warm against him, that he just couldn't help but lower his lips to hers. It would be a tough two years, keeping their kisses and loving caresses in public, as it was a strictly professional arrangement.

"You're such a charmer," she said, pushing at his chest playfully.

Their limo was waiting. Garrett escorted Willa to the open door, and she stepped inside. He followed in after her.

"You really do look beautiful," he told her.

"You clean up pretty good yourself." All he'd done was put on a suit, but Willa was in a class all her own. She looked beautiful, elegant, sexy—as she always did. When she settled into the seat, she crossed her long, shapely legs. Because of the high slit, the material of her dress shifted, exposing the delightfully smooth skin of her thigh. She cleared her throat, and he looked up, meeting her eyes, knowing he'd been caught staring.

Garrett forced himself to swallow, to bring up a new topic, lest he find himself indulging in his desire to see how far up that thigh he could go before he reached lingerie—*Is she a lace-panty woman? Satin?* He blew out a heavy breath, banishing those thoughts. "That wasn't so bad, was it?" he asked, finally. "We both survived."

"Mostly unscathed," she agreed. "How did your little chat with Thomas go?"

He shook his head. "Oh, forget about him. You know better than I do that he's an old blowhard."

"He is that. I'm kind of surprised that I got through the whole night without incident," she said with a laugh.

"Were you thinking of starting a fight with someone in your evening gown?"

She laughed, and he loved the sound of it. "Probably not. You know, despite the fact that Thomas was there, I had a nice time with your family," she said. "Seeing everyone come together to help a good cause. It was great seeing Daisy, too, and I'm glad that they were able to raise so much money for her clinic. No matter my opinion of most of the people of Applewood, they know how to open their checkbooks for a worthy cause."

It was true. Almost everyone in town went to Daisy for their pets and livestock, and they'd raised a large amount of money for the clinic. "And Daisy's the best," he added. "She does a lot of work for everyone in town."

"She's great. You're all lucky to have her."

"I'm glad you came with me," he told her. "You definitely made it more bearable."

"Thank you for inviting me," she said. Willa then settled into her seat before sitting up straight, shocked. "I totally forgot about Dylan. He came with us. Should we get him?"

Garrett shook his head. "Don't worry about him. Dylan told me he'd be getting a ride with someone else." Dylan had opted to get a ride with a woman he'd spent the entire night chatting up.

Willa rolled her eyes. "Of course, he did. You know, he doesn't seem too upset with the idea of us 'dating,'" she noted.

"Dylan's pretty laid back in general. But you're right. It could have gone a lot worse. Remember his threat to beat me up if I hurt you."

Willa turned serious and swiveled to face him. She placed her hand on his thigh. "Are you going to hurt me?"

He shook his head and put his hand over hers. "I never will."

A potent beat passed between them, and Willa looked away first. "Anyway," she said with an awkward laugh, "thanks again for tonight."

Garrett was grateful for the distraction, glad to be back on a safe topic. "See, I told you it wouldn't be all bad."

"I'm annoyed that you were right." Garrett noted

that she still hadn't moved her hand from under his. "Thanks for making me do this. And that dance we shared really distracted me. And that kiss."

She moved in closer, and he smoothed the hand he'd rested over hers up her arm, over her shoulder, to cup her cheek with his fingertips. He took her chin between his thumb and forefinger and drew her closer. Unable to help himself, he leaned in and touched his lips to hers. She gasped softly, then drew his breath into her mouth before relaxing and kissing him back.

She parted her lips, and her tongue snaked out, grazing his mouth. He pulled back. "I've been thinking about doing that again all night."

She nodded. "I've been thinking about that too."

"You have no idea how much I just wanted to do it again. Every time I've been with you." He leaned in and touched his lips to hers again. "I just want to touch you, kiss you."

"What about this being a fake relationship?" she asked him. "It's just a professional arrangement, right?"

Dammit, she was right. He pulled back a little, but he didn't stop touching her. "It is. I think I just got carried away."

"Me too. But that's okay. We can have this one kiss, right? Just this one time, and that's it?"

"Just to get it out of our systems?" he asked.

"Yeah. It has to work, right?"

"Can't see how it can fail."

After spending the entire time stationary in the

parking lot, waiting for its time to leave, the car finally began to move. He cursed the timing because he knew it was on its way to bring her back to Dylan's house, then him to his own. With desperation, he pulled her to him and kissed once more. She moaned into his mouth as his tongue explored hers, tasting her.

She reached her arms around his neck, and this time, pulled him to her. He pulled her across his lap so that her legs draped over his thighs. With their mouths together, parting only to breathe, he explored her with his hands.

He broke away from her, and it took both of them several seconds before their breathing returned to normal. But then he skimmed his lips against her jaw to her earlobe. "I can ask the driver to bring us both back to my place instead of dropping you off."

She shifted in his arms, and he reluctantly released her. He adjusted his pants, pulling at the material in his crotch. He'd never been so turned on, but she now showed tension in the way she bunched her shoulders and turned slightly away from him.

She shook her head. "I don't think that's a good idea," she told him.

"Why not?"

"This isn't a real relationship," she reminded him.

"That felt pretty real to me," he argued. Just a couple of minutes ago, they'd agreed to keep it platonic between them. That was what they would have to do. If only he could keep his goddamn hands to himself.

"We wanted to keep it simple, not confusing," she added.

"I think it's already too late for that."

Willa tried to force her heart rate to go lower as she steadied her breathing. The tension between them that had been building since he'd entered her life had been let loose. She couldn't believe what had just happened. She was supposed to be maintaining a friendly distance from Garrett. They were keeping it strictly professional. But she knew that getting too close was a danger to her. She needed to see this through; she had plans. But the way he'd touched her made her want to forget about every bit of common sense she possessed.

She thought about their agreement—she would pretend to be his girlfriend and he would give her the money to start her life over. She couldn't go to bed with him and screw it up for herself. No. She couldn't mix physical with professional. She was already in far too deep. There was no way to protect herself if she let herself get consumed by him.

"I don't know if I can do this anymore," she told him. "This is already too much for me."

"What do you mean?"

She realized how final she'd made it sound. "I'm not saying we have to end the arrangement. We need to see this marriage through. What I mean is we have to keep our distance. We can pretend to be a couple all we want, but this—" she waved her hands between them "—can't happen."

"I know. It's not smart," he told her, settling back into the other side of the car, giving her distance. "I can respect that. Maybe it would be best if we keep our hands to ourselves."

"I just think it'll make things easier for us if we keep it casual between us. Until the deal is done."

"You're right."

The interior of the car fell silent. Willa looked out the window and saw that they were turning up Dylan's driveway. The car stopped, and the driver came around and opened the door. If he'd known that things had turned X-rated in the back of the car, he didn't show it. As the driver helped her out of the limo, Garrett exited as well. "Let me walk you to the door."

He took her elbow to escort her to the door, and again, her eyes fluttered closed when he touched her. She had to hold steady in order to not invite him in. Even though Dylan would probably be out for the night and they would have the house to themselves, she couldn't let herself do it.

They stopped in front of the door and turned to face each other. "Thank you for a wonderful evening," Willa told him.

"Anytime. I just want to apologize for what just happened. I know you want to keep it platonic. I should have respected that."

In the light of the porch, he looked ruggedly handsome, his hair messy from her fingers. "Thank you. But I have to say, it was pretty incredible."

He smiled, and she had to stop herself from kissing him again. "It was, wasn't it?" He leaned in and kissed her cheek. "Good night, Willa," he said before backing away.

She was still standing on the front porch when the limo drove away, her mind swimming with her contradictory needs.

Six

Willa's phone was loud in her ear, waking her up the next morning. She groaned and rolled over. She hadn't slept more than a couple of hours the night before, and as the sun came up, she had fallen asleep with her phone in her hand, fingers at the ready to text Garrett for a last-minute bad-idea booty call.

"Hello?"

"Mornin', darlin'," he drawled in her ear. Speak of the devil.

"Garrett. Is anything wrong?" Her immediate thought went to Dylan. Ranches were dangerous workplaces, and she often worried about her brother.

"Nothing's wrong. Sorry if I'm calling a little early, but I wanted to catch you before you left to go home to High Pine."

"Oh yeah?"

"I meant to ask you this last night, but I got, uh, distracted. I was wondering if you wanted to join us tonight at our family barbecue. It's just something casual we do once a month."

She frowned. "It's pretty short notice," she said. "I only have the clothes I wore yesterday. And of course, my gown from last night. Not sure how suitable it would be for a barbecue."

"I wouldn't worry too much about that. You could wear what you wore to bed, and you would fit right in." Willa raised the blanket that covered her and looked down at her naked body. She didn't dare tell Garrett that she typically slept in the nude. "But anything you choose would look great."

The Hardwells were always welcoming, and she could easily slip back into the outfit she'd worn at work and go to the barbecue. She'd heard things about their legendary food spreads.

"Okay, I'll come. That sounds like a lot of fun. Thanks for inviting me." The offer warmed her. "I'll get ready. It'll be our first family function pretending we're together."

He paused. "Yeah. I guess it will. I thought it would be a good time to sow the seeds a bit that we're building a relationship. And I promise to keep my hands to myself this time."

She thought back to his hands and the way they'd touched her, and she felt a flush rise from her chest to her cheeks. She had no response to his comment, so she cleared her throat. "Okay, I guess I'll see you there."

* * *

Freshly showered and wearing a pair of jeans and a long tank top she'd found in her old dresser, she drove up the long, winding driveway to Hardwell Ranch. She parked her Mini next to a row of trucks—the obvious preferred vehicle of cowboys and ranchers in Texas. She walked up the porch steps and took a deep breath at the door.

Willa had seen most of the family at the fundraising gala the night before, but that didn't mean she wasn't nervous. To them, that had been her and Garrett's first date, but adding an invite to a family dinner—they were quickly entering "relationship territory." Which had been the plan, of course, she reminded herself. She and Garrett had to look like a couple, or at least lay the framework to look like they were one. She would have to spend the next two years of her life engaged in a charade, lying to their friends, their families and everyone they knew. Her life was about to become a lot more complicated. From here on out, things would be getting more and more serious. *More serious than that kiss last night in Garrett's limo?* she wondered, thinking about how much further they could have gone, feeling her core temperature rise in a way that had nothing to do with the Texas summer sun.

She took another deep breath and rang the doorbell, hearing the bell chime on the other side of the heavy oak door. The door opened, and she was surprised to see Elias on the other side. In Thomas's family, the housekeeper or butler was always responsible for opening the door. While she knew the main ranch house had a housekeeper, she was surprised to see the old man.

"Willa," Elias greeted her, surprised. "Seeing you twice in one weekend. What brings you by this evening?"

Cathy came up behind Elias, and seeing Willa, her eyes widened. She pushed forward, past Elias. "Is everything okay? Is something wrong with the save-the-dates?"

"No, nothing's wrong," she assured her. They were both looking at her expectantly, and Willa knew that she needed to say something else. "I'm here to—"

"Why don't y'all just leave the woman alone?" said a familiar voice from the hallway; it was Garrett's. "She's actually here to join us for the barbecue," he explained, coming up behind his grandfather and Cathy, earning him a surprised look from them both. "As my guest."

For several silent moments, the four of them stood in the foyer of the grand ranch house. Elias and Cathy both swiveled their heads back and forth, from Garrett to Willa to Garrett again, until Elias's gaze settled on Garrett and his eyes narrowed. "Willa is your guest?" he asked his grandson. "First the gala and then another date tonight. Is that right?"

Willa knew then that the old man was already onto them. He was sharp and would be able to see through them in a second, so they would have to make their act convincing. But for now, the two men were stuck in a standoff.

"That's right."

"It feels quick. Convenient."

"I don't know what you mean by that, but I sure don't like what you're implying."

Cathy pushed her way between the two men, reaching for Willa. "Well, both of you have forgotten your manners, it looks like. Get out of the way and invite her in," Cathy chided both men, pulling Willa farther into the house.

Garrett moved closer to her, put his hand on her lower back and drew her near. He kissed her on the cheek. "Thank you for coming," he whispered.

The kiss and his nearness had been unexpected, and she almost lost her breath. "Thank you for the invitation."

Thankfully, Elias and Cathy exited the foyer, leaving them alone. "So what's the assignment here tonight? Pretend I'm madly in love with you in front of your family?"

"What if you didn't have to pretend?" he teased, but then he turned serious. "But let's not lay it on too thick tonight. We're just setting the framework. No need to go overboard. Let's be friendly."

"But close."

"That's right."

"Can't be too much, too soon."

"Exactly." He paused. "Oh, by the way, your brother is here too."

She shouldn't have been surprised—Dylan was obviously close to all the Hardwells. She hadn't seen him that morning before he'd gone to the ranch, nor had they discussed her new relationship with his best friend. He didn't seem to have too much of a problem with it, which certainly made it easier to go through with the charade.

"Did he say anything about last night? Us being at the gala together?"

Garrett looked over his shoulder and toward the living room, where she could hear the rest of the family had gathered. "Nothing in particular. But he seemed fine with it last night."

She was glad that Dylan wasn't giving them a hard time. It was already hard enough having to lie to him, but Dylan being upset about it would make it so much harder. "How are you feeling about this? The gala went well. But this is going to be different. Smaller quarters," she said. "Close family. Your grandfather is probably already scrutinizing us."

"You noticed that too?"

"Kind of hard not to."

He reached out and put his hands on her upper arms, garnering her attention. "I know it's hard, and I'd like to say it's going to get easier, but it probably won't. The longer this goes on, the closer he'll be watching us."

She gave a lopsided smile. "Great pep talk, coach."

He laughed. "It'll all be worth it in the end."

"Yeah, the ranch will be yours."

"And a check will be in your hands."

As if he'd known they were talking about him, Dylan entered the foyer. "Will, I thought I heard you out here."

She stepped away from Garrett and toward her brother. "You were gone before I woke up this morning."

He smiled. "Yeah, I had some things to take care of here. I'm surprised to see you here. But I'm glad. I hope you're hungry, there's a lot of food."

"I'm starving," she told him. "Especially since you don't keep anything but old pizza boxes in your fridge. Have you ever heard of a grocery store?"

"Why buy groceries when all of my favorite restaurants will give me food?" They all shared a laugh before he looked between the two of them and hooked a thumb over his shoulder. "I'm going to head back inside."

Willa reached out and put a hand on her brother's forearm. "Wait, Dylan. Can we go outside and talk for a bit?"

"Yeah, sure."

She looked at Garrett. "Mind excusing us?"

That seemed to surprise him, as told by his raised eyebrows. "You okay?"

"Yeah, I'm fine. I just want to talk to my brother."

He looked between Willa and Dylan and nodded. "Sure. Meet me in the dining room when you're done."

"Will do."

When they were alone on the front porch, Willa turned to her brother. "I feel like it's been forever since we've talked. We haven't been spending much time together lately."

"I know. I've been really busy here, making way for the ranch's succession to Garrett and then getting things ready for all of the Hardwells who are coming to work for a while."

"Sounds like a lot to do," she said, sitting on the railing.

"We'll get through it." His eyes shifted toward the still-open door. "What's new with you?"

"You know how it is. Work, work, work." While summer was the most popular wedding season in many areas of the country, in Texas, one of the most popular seasons to get married in was fall. "I've got several weddings coming up in the next few months."

"Yeah, and your new love life is taking up a lot of time as well."

She knew that she and Dylan had to have a conversation at some point. Willa was at a crossroads. What should she tell him? Should she confess that they were not really together or go along with the charade and tell him that it was for real? He didn't seem to be upset that she and Garrett were spending time together…

Willa went with the lie.

"How exactly do you feel about it?"

Dylan's smile was uneasy, like he was embarrassed about the topic. He rubbed the back of his neck. "I only want the best for you. I want you to be happy. Does Garrett make you happy?"

"Yeah, he does."

"He's been my friend since we were kids. He's a great guy. If you're happy, then I'm happy. You could do a lot worse. Hell, you've *done* a lot worse. I've been worried about you," he confessed. "Maybe if you're with Garrett, I won't have to worry so much."

Willa smiled, but she still felt sad. She hated lying to her brother. She just had to trust it would all be worth it in the end. "I appreciate your concern," she told him. "But I'm grown. You don't have to worry about me."

"Will, I'm always going to worry about you."

She reached out and pulled Dylan in for a hug. "Thank you."

"For what?" he asked, when they separated.

She shrugged. "For being an incredible older brother. I couldn't have gotten this far without you."

"I didn't do anything," he told her. "You were the best little sister."

"Okay, we'd better get in there before this turns even more sappy."

"Yes, please," he said gratefully.

As they walked into the home, the foyer opened up into a large main room where people gathered. Off the main room, one short hallway led to the kitchen, another to the dining room. There was a cozy library in the back through another, and Elias's study sat opposite. A stone fireplace took up most of one wall, and in front of it sat a buttery-smooth, plush, chocolate-colored leather couch and two end chairs. The house was impressive, but the most spectacular feature, however, was the large glass wall that overlooked much of the rolling hills of the ranch. Outside, she also knew there to be a hot tub and pool built into the deck. The sun was getting low and had begun to cast an orange glow through the glass and onto the partygoers.

She had always loved the main house of the ranch. The home had been in the family for generations, and many of the fixtures and furnishings had been updated throughout the years. Expensive one-of-a-kind light fixtures lit the open room, and hundred-year-old furniture mixed with newer, plush, buttery-soft leather items. Despite the age of the place, the wood was shiny and well taken care of but still held the character and bore the marks of age and hard work from daily ranch life. She knew that rugs covered scuff marks on the floor. She noticed the series of marks on the kitchen wall where different generations of Hardwells had marked the heights of their children as they'd grown. The Hardwells had more money than most, and their family home was opulent and elegant—unlike what most have ever seen—but they were still a close, loving family. And that was what tugged at her heartstrings the hardest. She had never had anything like that. She had her brother, and they loved each other fiercely; but she'd never known the all-encompassing, unconditional, smothering love of a big family. The Hardwells were lucky, but it had nothing to do with their money or assets.

She'd known that Elias loved throwing a good party. But when Garrett had invited her to a barbecue, this wasn't exactly the scene she'd expected. Looking around, she could see that most of the ranch employees were there, and many greeted her and Dylan as they walked through the party. Through the glass wall, she could see people behind several grills; she could smell the charcoal and hear the sizzle. She was surprised to see that even a barbecue at the Hardwell ranch was a catered affair. Staff from an Austin barbecue restaurant—as told by their branded T-shirts—manned the grill while servers passed trays of appetizers. "This is a barbecue? It's quite a bit more than I'd expected."

Dylan laughed. "This is your first Hardwell barbecue. This is what they do."

"It's a bit much," Garrett said, coming up behind them. He handed each of them a beer that he'd likely picked up from the bar set up along a far wall. "Honestly, I would rather be at my own place, manning the steaks on my own grill. These barbecues started small, with a couple of men on the grill, the women doing everything else. But as the ranch expanded, we started inviting all the hands and their partners, and it then became a lot more work for everyone.

"We soon realized it's a lot more fun when we aren't all fighting over who gets to grill and the job they're doing. These nights are a lot more relaxed when we get someone else to do the actual work, and we can all spend the rest of night together. It might not be the way everyone else does it, but with how involved we all are with the ranch, we work every day. Really, who has the time?"

"It's nice that you all still find the time to spend with your family and treat the employees." She noticed that Dylan had drifted away and was now standing with a group she recognized as some senior ranch hands, leaving her and Garrett alone.

"Everyone works so hard," he told her. "They deserve it."

Willa sipped her beer and smiled up at Garrett. For how rugged Garrett was, he certainly enjoyed the finer things in life. He wrapped his arm around her shoulder, grazing her upper arm with his rough fingers. She inhaled and took in the scent of his cologne: woodsy, with a hint of citrus—definitely expensive. The rancher with a taste for luxury. She hadn't realized that the man was a study in contrasts.

"All right. We're on," he said. "Are you ready? Let's look like a couple for these people. Just pretend you like me and that I'm charming, funny, handsome…"

Willa knew she wouldn't have to work very hard at pretending. As if he'd said something hilarious, she laughed loudly and put her hand on his chest. It garnered some attention from those nearby. They watched her and Garrett for a second before turning back to their own conversations. "Like that?" she whispered.

"It's a start. But be careful—everyone here knows I'm not *that* funny."

She laughed again; this time it was genuine. "All right, let's do this."

He ushered her outside to the pool area, where Elias, Cathy, his father and stepmother, and family friends, including Dylan, were gathered. It would have been impossible for them to miss the way he held her, kept her close, and they attracted some questioning looks. She normally shied away from attention, but this charade was all about attention. She looked at Garrett and saw that he was looking down at her, and she smiled. Squaring her shoulders and holding her head high, she wrapped her arm around Garrett's waist. Pretending that she was falling for Garrett? That would be the easy part. The hard part would come later, after she'd already fallen.

With his arm around Willa—and trying to forget the last time he'd had his hands on her, the night before, in the limousine—Garrett led them to where his father and stepmother were standing. Stuart Hardwell had not been interested in working the ranch and had instead excelled in school and gone on to become the town's doctor. Garrett's mother, Ada, had passed away when he and his brothers were young. It wasn't until they were in their teens that his father had remarried.

"Dad, Elenore, you remember Willa, Dylan's sister?" He introduced them. "Willa, this is my father, Stuart, and his wife, Elenore."

"Yes," Stuart said, extending his hand to her, which she shook. "Of course. You're also the wedding planner."

"Event coordinator," Garrett supplied.

Willa and his parents made small talk for a while, but Garrett barely heard any of the words they were saying. His attention was captured by Willa as he looked down at her. The sheen of her hair, the delicate curve of her cheekbone, the dimple that appeared in her left cheek when she smiled—all distractions that were too much for him. She laughed at something his dad said, and his eyes dropped to her full lips. She'd applied some gloss to them, and he wondered if he kissed her right now, would she push him away?

He was brought back to their kiss the night before. He'd come so close to losing complete control. He could have had her right there in the limo, and it had taken all his restraint to not follow her to Dylan's door and beg to be let in. His stomach tightened with desire, and he knew that even though they'd agreed on keeping their hands and lips off each other—and that the night before had been an aberration, one they wouldn't repeat—he was now sure he wouldn't be able to stick to that agreement.

His hand was still on her lower back, and he moved it up and down her spine. He thought she might stiffen, but instead she softened slightly against him. His fingertip hit the strap of her bra, and he thought about sliding his finger beneath it. He removed his hand instead and took a step back from her. She noticed and looked up at him. The sunlight shining on her glossed lips was almost too much for him. "I've got to head inside for a bit. I'll be right back."

"Want me to come with?" she asked.

"No," he said too quickly. "It's fine. Stay out here. Enjoy the sunset." He headed inside, eager to get away from Willa before he put her over his shoulder and brought her to his bedroom in his own house. He needed a minute to clear his head, but before he could do that, he ran into Dylan.

"So, you made another date with my sister?" he asked.

"Yeah," he said. "I'm not sure this really counts as a date, but I wanted her to be here." Dylan nodded and drank his beer. "Are you mad?"

"No, I'm not mad. I gave you my blessing. But I want you to be honest with me when it comes to all of this. And her. It would kill me to see her hurt again. She's been through a lot."

"I know." He clapped a hand on Dylan's shoulder. "I'm not here to hurt anyone."

"I'm just afraid that she's going to fall for you, and you won't be able to return the favor."

Garrett could understand his friend's brotherly concern. "You don't have to worry. She's in good hands," he assured him. Garrett toyed briefly with telling Dylan the truth, but finally decided not to—he didn't think entangling his sister in a two-year charade would make him feel better about it. And he certainly didn't want to mix anyone else up in the scheme.

Dylan finally smiled. "I know she is." He turned and walked away, leaving Garrett standing alone. He felt bad about lying to his friend, but it was easier this way, for everyone. He looked out on the patio and saw that Willa was still talking to his dad, but Cathy and Elias had joined them. As if she could feel his gaze through the glass, she looked up and saw him. She waved. Garrett waved back. She looked beautiful in the orange glow of the setting sun. All he could think about was touching her, kissing her… Garrett exhaled heavily and knew he would have no trouble pretending to be attracted to her. Dylan had had it wrong. The issue wasn't Willa falling for him—because it seemed like she was able to keep her head on straight. It was himself he was worried about. Garrett was already up to his neck in it.

They passed the evening eating, drinking, touching, sharing looks. They didn't push it too far and weren't too over-the-top. Everyone was falling for their act already. Even Dylan seemed to be in good spirits.

The barbecue had been served, and as the catering team began their cleanup, the closer members of the family had gathered in front of the fireplace. Willa was perched on the large, thick arm of the leather chair where Garrett sat. His arm lay casually over her legs.

It was good to see him acting like himself again. Garrett's demeanor had shifted abruptly that evening. One moment, he'd been stroking her back, and then the next, he'd stepped away, but then he'd softened again. She hadn't questioned it, however, remembering that this whole thing was new to them both.

"Who wants coffee?" Cathy asked, standing. "I think I need a cup." Several people agreed that they would like some, and she turned to Willa. "Honey, would you like to give me a hand?"

"Of course. I'd love to."

"Cathy, she's a guest," Garrett said. "I'll go."

Willa put a hand on his shoulder. "Don't worry about it. I'll go."

Willa should have known that this wasn't just a trip to the kitchen to get coffee, because when they were out of the room and had reached the hallway leading to the kitchen, Cathy turned to her. "Can I ask what's going on here?" Cathy asked her, an interested glimmer in her eye.

She'd hoped to get away from any sort of interrogation, but no such luck, apparently. Willa almost caught herself explaining that *we're just friends*, but she stopped herself, remembering that she was supposed to be playing the role of the new lady in her step-grandson's life. She played it coy. "Oh, it's really nothing yet," she started. "Garrett and I reconnected a little at the engagement party. And then he needed a date to the gala, so he asked me."

"And tonight?"

She shrugged. "I guess it's just that I've been around the ranch so much lately during our meetings."

Cathy put her hand to her mouth. "Oh dear, yes. Pardon my bad manners. Perhaps I should have invited you myself. But I'm glad Garrett did. But, really, you have to tell me—just between us girls—is there something *romantic*—" she drew out the word "—between the two of you?" When she didn't answer right away, Cathy looked sheepish. "Oh, honey, I'm so sorry if I embarrassed you."

Willa played along, being careful not to do too

much. "It's not anything romantic. Not yet, anyway," she teased.

Cathy was intrigued again. "As if there might be something romantic soon?"

Willa smiled. "I think it's too soon to tell, but I do know that I like Garrett. I guess we'll just have to see what happens." It wasn't a lie; she did like Garrett. *Possibly too much*, she worried.

"I think I know just what will happen," Cathy said with a wink. "Maybe the next wedding you'll be planning will be your own."

Willa said nothing as Cathy busied herself getting the coffee ready. There *would* be a wedding coming sometime soon, but she hadn't thought about the actual time and energy that went into planning one for herself. It would be an extra commitment on top of her job and everything else in her life.

"I should have known this little trip to the kitchen wasn't just about getting coffee," Garrett said from behind her. She looked at the time and saw how late it was getting. She stifled a yawn.

"Tired?"

"Yeah, a little. We were out late last night."

He frowned. "You aren't heading back to High Pine tonight, are you?"

"No. I'm staying at Dylan's."

Garrett shook his head and blew out a heavy breath. "Why don't you let me bring you home?" he asked.

"I drove my car here," she reminded him. "I'm fine. I'm not too tired to drive."

They both knew that Cathy was watching them

carefully from the pantry, so in a move that was no doubt for her benefit, Garrett put his hands on Willa's waist and pulled her close. "Why don't we go for a short walk instead? The fresh air will wake you up a bit, and—" he leaned close "—I haven't had much of an opportunity to have you to myself tonight."

Willa was tired and was looking forward to hitting the hay, but the specific tone of Garrett's voice made her want to walk the entire length of the expansive 2500-acre ranch with him.

"That sounds nice."

He led her to the back door, and they let themselves out. The sky was clear, and the moon and stars lit their way. The night air was quiet and fresh. She took a deep breath, pulling it into her body, becoming refreshed.

"Thank you for everything tonight," he said, taking her hand. The gesture surprised her because they'd agreed on being platonic when there was no one else around. But Willa went with it. She liked the way her hand felt in his. "I really appreciate you doing this for me."

"Do you think people bought it?" she asked him.

"We're on the right track. I think we've been pretty convincing. You were great."

"So were you."

They walked in silence for a while. She listened to the sounds of the ranch. She could hear the rustling of the horses in their stalls and the cattle herds nearby. The soft breeze rustled the branches, and owls and nocturnal animals woke up, calling out around her. She inhaled the warm, sweet nighttime air and smiled. It had been a while since she'd been happy in Applewood, but walking hand in hand with Garrett by the light of the moon brought her pretty damn close.

When he sighed, she looked up at him. "You okay?"

"Yeah, I'm just thinking."

So she was alone in enjoying the quiet, relaxing stroll? "What about?"

"Elias, this whole thing," he started. "I can't believe that I have to be doing this. How can he make me jump through these damn hoops? I thought that spending my entire life devoted to this place would be enough to make it mine when he steps down. Hell, Wes has only been back to Applewood a handful of times since he moved to California. And Noah would rather be in his beachside hut in the Keys with his paintings than be here. And then there's the rest of my cousins—where have they been? I'm the one who's been living and breathing this place since I was a kid."

Willa knew that Elias's terms had been frustrating to Garrett, but she wondered if he'd ever told anyone as such. She let him vent, knowing it was something he needed to do. "You know," she started, "maybe that's it. Maybe he doesn't want you to *live and breathe* the ranch. He wants to encourage you to get away and find some time for fun and love, and look for the other things in life."

He looked down at her. She could see his grin in the moonlight. "Believe me, I have no trouble finding the fun things," he quipped.

"But he's old-fashioned. He was lucky enough to find love for a second time. Maybe he wants you to find it once."

"Do you think that's everything there is to life? Love and fun?"

"It's more than working from dusk to dawn, I guess. But in my professional opinion, I'd say yes. They say love is the most important thing in life." She paused. "Honestly, though, love has never really worked out for me."

"Thomas," he said.

"Not just Thomas," she confided. "You know my background. No real family to call my own. Dylan's really the only person I've loved and trusted." He squeezed her hand, the simple gesture making her swallow a sigh. "That's what makes this tough for me. I hate lying to him." Willa shook her head and tried to get back to a fun place with Garrett. "Okay, enough of all of that. I really did have a fun night, though. I love your family. Thanks for inviting me."

"I'm glad you came. I think we put on a pretty good show of being attracted to each other, don't you?" He paused. "Unless it wasn't an act," he prodded.

They'd circled back and came to stop next to her car, which she'd parked next to Garrett's truck. But instead of letting her say good-night and get into her car, he drew closer. His fingertips touched her waist. Unable to stop her reaction, she stepped closer to him. They were alone, and the closeness was not for the benefit of anyone else. Willa knew this was yet another moment that was strictly for them.

When she didn't respond right away, he moved in more, his palms flattening on her waist and smoothing to her back, settling on the curve above her behind. "Was it an act, Willa?"

"Not totally," she confessed. "It was a lot of fun. It felt natural."

"It did for me too."

He leaned in, and his lips grazed against hers, and she caught his top one between them for a quick, soft nip. He pulled back and smiled before going in for another kiss. This time, she was ready for it and met him halfway. Their lips parted, and their tongues met. She wrapped her arms around his neck, unable to do anything but pull him closer.

He raised his hands to her front, and he found her full breasts, cupping and squeezing her through the material of her shirt. She knew they were in front of the ranch house and would be exposed to anyone who walked outside, but still, she arched into his touch. His hands went underneath her shirt, and he sought out her nipples, which were rigid, raised under her lace bra.

Garrett dropped his hands to the zipper of her jeans and pushed them down her thighs. She thought that his jeans would come next, but instead, he toyed with the band of her panties. Every bit of tortured, unreleased energy from the night before pulsated through her body. Every part of her throbbed in need for Garrett.

"Is this what you want?" he asked.

"Yes," she answered, completely breathless.

He grinned and pulled her closer.

They might have both missed the door of the main house opening if Dylan hadn't called "Thanks for the barbecue," to whoever had walked him outside.

"Oh God, it's Dylan," Willa gasped, pulling her jeans up as Garrett adjusted himself in his.

"Dammit," Garrett cursed under his breath as Dylan unwittingly came closer to them.

"Garrett? Willa, is that you?" he said in the darkness.

"Yeah, hey, man," Garrett greeted him. "You heading home?"

"Yeah. What are you guys doing out here?"

"We just went for a short walk," Willa explained. "I was just heading home."

"Yeah, me too." He slapped his thigh. "I just remembered—I left my truck over by the western pasture. Can I get a ride with you?"

"Yeah, of course." She opened the driver's-side door and looked up at Garrett.

She had no doubt about what would have happened between them if Dylan hadn't come along. It was confusing. They'd both agreed that they would keep their hands to themselves, but there was something about their chemistry that made her helpless when it came to Garrett. If the past two nights had been any indication, that was going to be easier said than done.

Seven

Garrett was dressed before the sun came up that morning. His work normally had him waking up with the roosters, but normally he'd been able to have a good night's sleep before. He grimaced as he pulled a white T-shirt over his head. Once he'd gotten home, it had taken a full thirty-minute cold shower before he could think about anything but Willa. He knew how things would have progressed last night, and he wasn't sure if he was grateful or disappointed that Dylan had shown up when he had. He liked Willa a lot, and there was no doubt he wanted to take her to bed, but if they had to stick this out for at least the next two years, he was going to have to control his urges.

After a restless night, Garrett decided on a ride

around the property. He saddled up his favorite horse. With a flick of the reins, he was off. He'd spent so much of his life on these very grounds. He knew every rolling hill, every dip and hole. He knew the smell, the perfect place to watch the sun rise. It was his ranch—and he wasn't going to let his grandfather give it to either of his brothers.

Several ranch hands were already up and at work. There was so much to do day and night on the ranch that he couldn't imagine where to find the time or energy to put toward a relationship. No woman wanted to play second fiddle to the land and the herds. That was initially why he'd thought a fake relationship would be the best way to play this. He didn't want to fall for a woman—or have her fall for him—just for it to fall apart because he couldn't nurture a real relationship.

As the sprawling land opened up around him, he thought of his walk with Willa the night before. If he wasn't careful, he would let himself start feeling for her, and then he could just blow this whole thing to hell. He shook his head with new resolve. It would be best if they kept the touching and kissing to a minimum, and did it only in public, when they were trying to sell the fake relationship. They needed to learn to keep their damn hands to themselves.

He came up over a hill to see Elias standing next to the southern-boundary fence. Garrett pulled up the reins to stop. He dismounted and tied her up next to his grandfather's horse.

"Some morning," Garrett said as he joined his

grandfather, who was leaning on the fence, watching the vista below them. The morning was still, serene.

"Sure is. Nothing like a calm, quiet morning."

They looked over the fence in silence, both men enjoying the stillness.

"Good barbecue last night," Garrett said.

Elias nodded. "It was. I'm glad everyone enjoyed it." He paused. "I was most surprised you invited a woman. You've never done that before."

Garrett had to play it cool and not make it seem to Elias that he and Willa were taking the too-much-too-fast approach. They were in the beginning phase of a relationship, so it had to look natural. "I was being nice. Willa's a good woman, and she's around here more often these days, planning your wedding and such."

Elias narrowed his eyes at Garrett. "Tell me, are you and Willa an item?"

And there it was. His grandfather was asking straight out. This would be the first time he'd lied to the man who'd taken him under his wing and showed him how to run a successful ranch. "We aren't label-ing it yet," he said, noncommittal.

"It's convenient timing," Elias noted. "Given my retirement announcement."

Garrett shrugged. "You wanted me to meet a woman, get married, didn't you?"

"Oh, you're going to marry her, now, are you?"

"I obviously don't know that yet," Garrett re-sponded. "We got reacquainted at your party the other night. Your conditions—*threats*—to hand the place over to Wes and Noah lit a fire under my ass, I guess. Do you want me to get married and fulfill your demands, or not?"

"I guess I do." Elias pointed a finger at him. "But listen here, son, I made those conditions, and you signed a legally binding contract that you would find a wife. But if I get even a whiff that you aren't taking this seriously, or faking the whole thing, it's done. There's no deal." Elias was always stern but loving. But he let his wishes be known.

Garrett nodded. "I signed it, didn't I?"

"Good. If you think what you may have with Willa is real, then I'll be happy for you. But if it isn't, and it's all a way to get the ranch quickly with fakery, then it's all over. I explained to you why this is so important to me. I want to see you fully experience life. It's not just about the business, and I want to make sure you do that before I leave all of this," he said, sweeping his arm around, showcasing their surroundings.

For so long, the ranch had been everything to Garrett. He hadn't known that there should be more. "How come you don't make these rules for Wes or Noah, or any of my cousins?"

"You know I've never been one to pick favorites," he explained. "But I've always been closest to you. I need to know that when I'm no longer around, you have everything you could have ever wanted."

Garrett finally understood. It wasn't about controlling Garrett's life. Elias just wanted to know that Garrett was truly happy before he moved on. This made Garrett feel terrible for lying to him. But there was no way he would go to Longhorn's or a dating app to find a woman. He didn't have time for that. Not when he had the perfect woman in his life already.

"I'm going to head back to the main house for breakfast," Elias said after several beats of silence. "Get a start on the day." He got back up on his horse, and Garrett noticed that his grandfather showed a little difficulty in doing it. Elias was getting on in years, and perhaps he'd realized he couldn't be a cowboy forever.

"Yeah, I'll meet you back there," he told him. "I'm going to ride for a bit. Some of the guys mended the fence. I want to check it out."

After watching his grandfather head down to the trail on his horse, Garrett mounted his own horse and rode on. Riding allowed him to clear his mind so he could think things through. But as he passed all the familiar landmarks, all he could think about was Willa. Despite everything he'd already told himself, how he vowed to keep things platonic with her, he'd already forgotten it. He had to see her again.

Eight

It was Monday morning, and Willa was at her desk, when her phone rang. She checked her caller ID and saw that it was Daisy. She smiled. She hadn't had a chance to talk to her friend much at the gala, as Daisy had been busy greeting donors. "Hello?"

"Hey, are you working in High Pine today?"

"I am."

"I'm coming in for some meetings. Want to get lunch?"

"Yeah, that sounds like fun. I'll make reservations."

"Great! I have to run now, but I'll text you later."

Willa disconnected the call, and using an app, made the reservations at one of her favorite local spots while her computer booted up. It would be nice to catch up, although Daisy was probably just interested in the latest gossip about her she'd no doubt heard at the clinic.

That suspicion was confirmed three hours later, when Daisy bustled into the restaurant.

"You complete beyotch," she said instead of any kind of standard greeting.

"*Hi* to you too."

"I cannot believe you didn't tell me, and I had to hear it from some old biddy who came in for flea treatment."

"I assume you mean she brought her *pet* in for a flea treatment."

"Funny. But don't think you're getting out of this conversation so easily." Daisy pursed her lips at her.

"What are you talking about?"

"You're officially dating Garrett Hardwell." Willa didn't say anything, so Daisy kept going. "I thought he was just a friend. I should have known something was up when you went to the fundraiser with him— thank him for his donation, by the way."

"How did you find out?" Willa asked.

"Please, you know that before the fundraiser was over, people were talking. I'm just upset you didn't come to me first."

Again, Willa was in a position of lying to someone she loved. She forced a smile. "Yeah, sorry, I meant to tell you. It just happened so quickly. We reconnected at the engagement party, then he asked me to the gala."

"And then the Hardwell-family barbecue," Daisy added.

"What, is someone writing a blog about me?" she asked.

"Pretty much." She dug into her bag and pulled out a copy of the *Applewood Tribune*. "And then there's this."

Willa took the newspaper from her, and just as she'd suspected, a picture of her and Garrett from the gala was featured. But not the one in front of the step-and-repeat banner—it was a picture of the moment Garrett had kissed her before going inside.

"Give me all the details."

"Unfortunately, there aren't any details to share, Daisy," she insisted. "We've only had a couple of dates. Not that those could be considered dates." She didn't mention what had happened between them after the barbecue, however. That was their secret.

"Come on. There's nothing to share? This is the juiciest thing to happen to me in a long time."

"Happen to *you*?"

"You know what I mean. But, come on, it's Garrett. And I'm in such a dry spell. Let me live vicariously through you."

Willa raised her hands in surrender. "Fine. He's a very good kisser, okay?" She could feel her heartbeat ratchet up a few notches thinking about his lips on hers.

"That's it? The guy's a good kisser?"

"Leave me alone. You're supposed to be my friend."

"If that was true, you would have surely told me about the hunky, *very rich* rancher it sounds like you've secretly been seeing."

"I haven't been secretly seeing anyone." In fact, it was quite the opposite. She was secretly *not seeing him*. "And now I'm once again the town curiosity." She wasn't surprised, but she should have known that the Applewood rumor mill churned 24/7, even on weekends. But at least, it might take people's attention over the tragedy that was her wedding day.

Daisy picked up the menu. "I wouldn't worry too much about that. You and Garrett are hot stuff now, but it'll blow over soon enough."

"I don't know," Willa said, shaking her head. "They still haven't forgotten about the last time I was hot stuff." Daisy gave her a sympathetic look, but Willa ignored it. She wanted to stop dwelling on the past, but it just kept popping back up when she least expected it. She thought about the next two years and how this speculation and gossip would be a huge part of her life. How long after that could she expect the blowback to last?

Nine

On Friday, Willa found herself once again driving back into Applewood. She hadn't intended to come back, but when she'd gotten home from work, she'd walked into her empty apartment and, for the first time, found the quiet uncomfortable. When she'd first moved to High Pine, she'd sought the solitude, but after spending all last weekend with her brother, and Garrett and his family, she had become used to being surrounded by people who loved and supported each other. She had no plans in High Pine this weekend, so she packed a bag and got back in her car.

When she turned into Dylan's driveway, she saw his truck parked near the back door of the house, and she parked next to it. She grabbed her bag and walked up the steps to the large patio they'd built together a few summers ago.

The door opened, and Dylan walked outside; it looked like he was on his way out. "Hey, Will," he said, surprise raising his eyebrows behind his sunglasses. "I didn't know you were coming today."

"Should I have called in advance?" she teased.

"Of course not," he said, wrapping his arms around her in a hug. "This place is as much your home as it is mine. You're always welcome here, especially since you've been here so often lately."

"Yeah, I have. You know I'm working on Cathy and Elias's wedding."

"I know Cathy can be demanding, but you don't show this amount of attention to your other clients."

"What's that supposed to mean?"

"Nothing at all. I'm a fan of anything that brings you home."

Home. When Dylan said it, she almost believed it.

"But, come on, Will. I know that work isn't the only reason you spend an awful lot of time in Applewood."

"And, pray tell, what's the reason?"

"It's Garrett."

She could say he had nothing to do with it, but after a week, she found herself missing the guy. It wasn't smart. How was she supposed to be keeping her distance—mentally and emotionally—if she couldn't go a week without seeing him? She said nothing.

"Do you guys have any plans?"

"No, we don't at all." They'd shared some text messages throughout the week, but they hadn't made any plans to meet up that weekend. She was in a weird position in the fake relationship. She knew they were supposed to be putting on a show. But she didn't want to appear too eager, and even though the danger of falling for him was real—especially with what had almost happened between them after the barbecue—she was starting to like him, and it was necessary to put up her boundaries to not completely lose herself. If he wanted to see her, he would let her know, but that didn't mean she couldn't make herself available. "He doesn't even know I'm here. Really, I just came because I got home to my apartment, and I felt lonely in High Pine. Yes, I have friends there, and no matter what people here think of me, I wanted to see you, and Daisy, and yes, Garrett. There was nowhere else I wanted to be."

They were still standing on the patio, and it looked like Dylan just realized it. "Oh, let's go inside."

"Thanks. You were on your way out. You don't need to stay and keep me company."

"I wasn't going anywhere important. Let's hang out. We can watch some old movies, make popcorn. Like the old days."

She smiled at her brother. "I'd like that."

The next afternoon, Willa was curled up on Dylan's porch with a book she'd been looking forward to finishing and a cup of coffee. That was another thing she'd grown to love about Applewood.

It was quieter; time somehow moved more slowly there. When she wasn't hyperfocused on work, she was able to fully relax.

She heard a vehicle approach and couldn't help but smile when she saw it was Garrett's truck. He parked and hopped down from the cab. He walked up the path but didn't climb the stairs to the porch. Instead, he stopped and rested his forearm on the railing.

"Heard you were in town," he said with a slow, sexy drawl as he removed his sunglasses.

"Word travels fast."

"Don't we know it. I guess you saw that picture in the paper."

"I did."

"You have any plans this afternoon?"

"Just me and Nora," she said, holding up her paperback.

"Tell her you'll see her tomorrow."

"Why? Do you have something in mind?" she asked.

"I was thinking about going for a ride," Garrett told her. "I've got some of the guys saddling up a couple of horses for me. Would you like to join me?"

"Yeah, I'd love to. Do you have any particular destination in mind? What should I wear?" she asked, looking down at the sleeveless-tunic-and-yoga-pants combo she'd put on after her shower.

"You're beautiful in what you're wearing. This definitely isn't anything fancy. It's just a simple ride."

That was a relief. Most of the times they'd gone out together were in public places—parties in town, family events. It felt strange that they were doing something more casual. "Okay, great. I guess I'm ready right now."

He extended his hand to her, and she put down her book and accepted it. They got in the truck for the short drive to the ranch. Strangely, they didn't make conversation on the way, but when they got out of the truck, Garrett took her hand, a part of the show for anyone they might happen along, and they strolled to Garrett's personal stable, where his horses were kept. Two horses were already saddled for them. "You rode a lot here when we were younger," he said. "How long has it been since you've been on a horse?"

The Hardwells had been her and Dylan's saviors when they were younger. They'd spent so much time on the ranch, Elias and the others showing them how to ride and providing distraction from their lives in their foster homes. "It's been a few years."

"You okay with your own horse?"

She imagined herself sharing a saddle with Garrett, her back pressed to his warm, strong chest, but she had to shake those images away, lest she feel herself falling too deeply. She had to remind herself that this relationship with Garrett wasn't real. It was a facade, a charade to fool everyone around them. She needed to remember that. It was a romantic notion, but she knew that she had to keep her distance. She couldn't let herself get too deep—well, deeper than she already had. "I can ride my own." Garrett extended his hand to her, and she took it and raised her leg to put her foot in the stirrup, then pulled herself up.

She caught him staring with an amused grin on his lips. "What?"

"You look really good up there. Like a real cowgirl."

"Yeehaw," she said with a wink.

"How does it feel?" Garrett asked, mounting his own horse. He sat up straight and held the reins in his strong hands. The man looked good on a horse, and he confidently commanded his own mount.

She grasped her reins, and the horse subtly reacted, as if it recognized that she was in control. "Like old times," she assured him.

"Just like riding a bike?"

"Well, you know, I had to get back on the horse someday," she joked.

They left the ranch property and rode through some horse trails that surrounded Applewood. Willa loved living in High Pine, but she missed the quiet solitude of the trails. They rode for more than an hour until they came to a familiar road.

"Come this way," Willa said, leading them down the narrow gravel road. When they came upon the property that held the mansion, she lightly pulled back the reins, enough to stop the horse.

He stopped next to her. "What are we doing here?"

"This place is my future."

"It's yours?"

"No. Not yet. It belongs to Thomas," she explained. "A few years ago, I did some research, and I learned that it originally belonged to my mother's family. But a while back, the ownership transferred to someone else. It was put up for sale, and it was on the market for so long that after talking with the owners, they offered to hold on to it until I could buy it from them. I made the mistake of sharing with Thomas that I wanted to buy it, and then after the wedding debacle, he bought it from under me."

"Why would he do that?"

"Just so I couldn't have it. Out of spite because I embarrassed him. Now he's doubled the price and told me I can have it if I pay him way over what it's worth, and—get this—he's adding monthly 'interest' to the amount until I can pay. He'd rather see the place rot than let me have it."

Garrett cursed under his breath. "That's despicable."

"That's Thomas. He knew that place was important to me. It's one of the only connections I have to the past."

"So, what do you want to do with it?" Garrett asked.

"I picture it as a small inn. Tourism is growing in the area. I know with the right renovations, it'll be a success." She sighed, thinking about the future she could have. "Maybe someday."

"That's what you studied at college, right? Hospitality and business?"

She smiled. "You remembered."

"Of course, I did." He was quiet for a bit. "How much money do you need?"

"Too much."

"Let me give you more. For our deal. I can give it to you now before Thomas sells it to someone else."

She held up a hand. "No, don't. I won't accept any more charity."

"It's not charity. Listen, you're doing me a favor. But I can write you a check right now and help make this happen for you. We agreed I was going to pay you for marrying me."

Willa had to admit, it was tempting. How easy it would be to just take his money. But no, she wouldn't make herself weak or beholden to another man. He'd agreed to pay her the amount after their wedding, that was their deal. She didn't want to have to owe Garrett any more favors. That was how things had gone so off the rails with Thomas. He'd had more money than she had, more power and influence. She should have seen the signs, and when she'd found the scandalous pictures from another woman, she hadn't had the time to confront him about them, and she hadn't had the agency to stop herself from walking down the aisle. But it was at the altar where she'd had a moment of clarity that if she had gone through with it, she would have never been happy. So, she did the only thing she could; she walked—okay, she ran—away.

"Tell me. How much do you need?"

Finally, she told him the amount. "But that's just to start. It needs some extensive work to make it spectacular. And then there's my debt to consider. I'm still paying for the wedding to Thomas."

That earned her a look from him. "*You're* paying

for the wedding? Thomas and his family have more than enough to take care of it."

"I thought it had been paid for. Thomas was supposed to take care of it. But it was after I left him at the altar that all of the bills came in. They were in my name. And I'd rather die than go back to him for money. So I've been paying down the debt. I decided then that I would never depend on a man for anything—financially, emotionally or otherwise."

Garrett shook his head in disgust. "That's the money he says you tried to extort from him. I had no idea. It must be so tough for you."

"That's why I left town. I could barely show my face around here without the stares and the whispers. It killed me because Dylan was here, and my friends. I drove into High Pine without a place to stay or a job, and a little bit of *screw-you* cash in the bank."

"'*Screw-you* cash'?" he asked.

She shrugged. "Just some money I saved up while I was with Thomas. Something I did in case things went south." She stopped and thought about it. "Maybe that was a sign that I knew it wouldn't work out. I made sure to have enough money to get away from him. As much good as that did me." She couldn't believe that she was telling Garrett all this. She felt vulnerable, and that was a feeling she wanted to avoid. After telling Thomas about the house, he'd screwed her over, and she had vowed then that from there on, she would only rely on herself. But telling Garrett had been so easy.

"It's always good to be prepared." His eyes were

on the darkening sky. The sun was beginning its descent. "Speaking of, it's getting late. We should get back." They turned their horses back toward the ranch.

They rode in silence for a while before he spoke again. "So what happened after you arrived in High Pine—without a job or a home, and one of those sacks with a dollar sign painted on it, filled with *screw-you* cash?"

She laughed, glad he was trying to lighten the mood after a serious conversation. "I checked online apartment ads from my car and chose the first place I visited. The next day, I found the job with Miriam. Everything just kind of worked out from there."

"Do you like your job?"

Her laugh was humorless. "It's okay. But I'm an event coordinator who only gets assigned to work on weddings. Like it's some sick karmic joke because I walked out on my own."

"Ouch."

She shook her head roughly. "I can't believe I'm out here unloading everything on you. I'm sorry. I didn't want to tell you all of this. I'm afraid I've ruined a great ride."

"You didn't ruin anything," Garrett assured her. "Thank you for sharing. I'm glad you told me."

She hadn't meant to tell him any of those things. "I know that this is only a fake relationship, but I'm glad I told you too. You're easy to talk to."

"So are you."

When they arrived at Hardwell Ranch, they rode

to the stables. Garrett dismounted first and helped her from her own horse before they handed them off to a ranch hand who would put them in for the night.

"That was great," she told him. "Thank you. It was awesome to get back on a horse and explore nature."

"Thanks for coming out with me. I don't often get to go on leisurely rides with beautiful women."

"I don't know about that," she said. "I'm sure there are many women who would go with you."

"But none of them are my future wife."

"You're right. You know, this whole day, I kind of forgot about our arrangement." It had just been the two of them all afternoon. The ride had felt more like a date than anything they'd done yet—it was intimate, they'd shared and they'd done so without an audience.

"Me too," he said with a smile. "Normally, I just ride by myself. I like the solitude, and it helps me clear my head. But I'm glad we did it together."

"Me too." She knew that she was supposed to be keeping her distance, but she literally felt herself gravitating toward him, getting closer. Before she could stop herself, she said the words that she should have swallowed. "Do you have any plans tonight? We could get dinner."

"Darlin', I'd love nothing more than to say no. But Elias and I are heading to Fort Worth for a rodeo."

Deflated, she nodded. She guessed it would be another night of movies and snacks on Dylan's couch. "That sounds fun." She didn't want to appear desperate. This wasn't a real relationship. To Garrett, she knew that this was an arrangement where he would just text her if he needed a date.

"Trust me, I would much rather do whatever you had in mind when you asked."

She had to disengage from this conversation. She'd already revealed so much about herself that afternoon that she didn't want to make herself look desperate for his attention. "Oh, it was nothing." Stupid. This was exactly what he'd warned her about. The ranch would always be his priority. Not a relationship. "We both have to eat, right? If you need your fake girlfriend for anything else, just give me a call, and I can come to Applewood."

He must have noticed her change in demeanor. "Thanks for the offer. Is everything okay?"

"Yeah, why wouldn't it be?" She didn't give him time to respond. "I'd better let you go get ready for your trip to Fort Worth," she said. "Can you give me a ride back to Dylan's?"

Ten

When Cathy had learned that Willa had come to town, she'd insisted on a Monday-morning meeting to go over some ideas for the ceremony venue before she went back to High Pine. For the amount of time Willa spent in Applewood, she figured she might as well move back. *Hah! No chance of that!* she laughed to herself. Sure, she'd spent the weekend wrapped in a still, comfortable small-town cocoon, but after her embarrassing display of asking Garrett to dinner and getting shot down, she realized that she'd been an idiot. It reminded her that she and Garrett weren't really building a relationship, and that when there was no one around, he would always consider her just an acquaintance. He'd even told her when they'd started that he would always put the ranch first. He'd given her a fair warning, and she hadn't heeded it. But one thing Willa knew was that she would never be with a man who didn't make her a priority.

As she sat on Dylan's couch—alone on a Saturday evening, watching Julia Roberts pretend to be Richard Gere's girlfriend for a week—she knew that it wouldn't work out like that for her. She would be Garrett's wife, but it would be all business. No climbing the fire escape or declarations of undying love. After the two years was up, their ending would be a quick annulment and a check. Which was fine with her.

She knew exactly where Cathy was leading her. She'd imagined that the trail to the old swimming hole would be overgrown, but it was surprisingly manicured. When they came to the secluded clearing, Willa smiled as the memories came flooding back. At the end of the trail was a small waterfall that emptied into a round pool and connected stream. She, Dylan and Garrett used to swim and fish there as kids, but what she remembered was the way, upon sunset, the sun would fall over the distant hills, creating the most beautiful skies she'd ever seen.

It was also the very place, where she and Garrett had slept together that night more than a decade ago. They'd gone to the secluded spot to watch a meteor shower. He'd laid a blanket, and she'd smuggled a bottle of wine from Patsy's Diner. They'd gotten tipsy and watching the stars had turned to kisses, and then led to much, much more…

"You know, in my few years living here on the

ranch, I've barely been down here myself," Cathy said, pulling Willa from her trip down memory lane.

"The ranch is so expansive, it would be hard for one to explore its every corner and cranny."

Willa looked up to see Garrett approach. It was no surprise that she would run in to him; the ranch was his home, after all. He was on horseback, and she had forgotten what a fine figure he cut on a horse. With the reins in his firm, capable hands, he commanded the animal with grace that belied his rugged exterior.

"It is absolutely stunning here," Cathy said. "I want our event to be small but tasteful. It's the second wedding for both of us."

"There's no reason why you can't do everything you've ever wanted," Willa reminded her. "We could have the ceremony here, and even flip it in time to have the reception here also."

"Oh, I love it here so much."

"We would just have to work out the logistics for getting the food and band down here."

She had expected Garrett to pass right on by them. But instead, he came to a stop in front of them. After saying hello to Cathy, he turned to Willa. "Can I talk to you?"

"Yeah, of course. I'll be right back," she told Cathy.

He tied his horse to a nearby post, and they walked to a small toolshed that was nearby. They went around the back so that they could have some privacy. "It looks amazing down by the stream."

"Yeah, I fixed it up a few years back. I like to go down there every now and then."

"You did?" She wondered if the small piece of land held the importance to him that it did to her. But no, she told herself. It wasn't like that night so many years ago held any significance to him. "I think we might have the wedding down there. It's beautiful."

He removed his hat and pushed his fingers through his hair. "I feel like I did something to upset you on Saturday."

"No, don't worry about it."

"I'd had those plans with Elias. We were special guests. If I led you on—"

"You didn't. We had a nice time on our ride. I was just kind of hungry and thought you might be too."

"I told you that this is what I do," he reminded her. "The ranch and the business are my priority."

"I know, and I get that."

"Okay. How would you like to come back to Applewood next weekend?"

"Why?"

"Cathy and Elias want to take us to dinner on Friday. I know he just wants to watch us up close, to make sure we're actually a couple, so we'll have to be convincing."

"I can do that. I'll drive out after work on Friday. I'll tell Dylan to expect me."

"That's another thing. I'd like you to stay at my place."

"Oh really?"

"You can stay in my guest room, of course. But

I feel like it's time to take it to the next level." Her eyes shot to his, and he continued. "Not like that, of course," he assured her.

"Okay," she agreed. "That's something I can do."

"Send me a list of your favorite foods and necessities. I'll make sure my housekeeper has everything you need."

She nodded. "Anything else I have to know about this dinner?"

"Not really. Like always, we just need to put on a show that we're crazy about each other, pretend that we can't keep our hands off each other."

Willa didn't need to pretend, but she didn't say as much. "I can do that, I think," she said.

"Good," Garrett murmured, taking a step closer to her. "But I'm right here if you think you need some practice." He reached for her, and she allowed him to pull her into his embrace.

"There's nothing wrong with a little practice," she whispered, unable to help herself as her palms slid up his torso. His chest was warm, firm, and his arms were strong, wrapped around her. Despite herself, and against every bit of willpower she had to keep the arrangement, to protect herself, she looked up at him. His eyes were on her, and before she could push away from him, his lips lowered to meet hers.

His lips were full, firm and fully confident. She and Garrett had kissed before, but this felt different. Urgent. As his palms explored up and down her back, before threatening to dip lower, she fell into the kiss and his embrace. She parted her lips, and he deepened the kiss and pulled her closer. The way he felt, the way he tasted, the way he smelled—the mingling of soap, outdoors and his desire—triggered every one of her senses.

Garrett wrapped his arms around her waist and lifted her, pinning her between his strong chest and the rough exterior of the shed. It might have been ruining the fine material of her blouse, but that couldn't have been further from her mind. In fact, she wouldn't even care if he ripped it from her body.

With her legs spread, wrapped around Garrett's waist, her skirt bunched at her hips; and even though he was kissing her like he needed her mouth to survive, Garrett noticed. He drew his fingers along the strip of satin that separated him from her core. Just that simple, most intimate touch forced a gasp from her throat. But when he pushed her panties aside, she couldn't hold back. She arched her back and flexed her hips against him, wordlessly urging him on. "So hot," he whispered against her lips with a grin.

He slid his fingers along her most needy spot, and she gave a loud cry before he dipped his fingers inside her. Despite every promise she'd made to tell herself that she would not let this get out of control, she needed this. She craved his touch, and she never wanted him to stop. He grunted in her ear, a rough noise so primal that it sent a shiver down her spine as she ground against him, wanting more, needing more.

Supporting her, keeping her up with one arm, he used his hand to bring her to a height of pleasure she'd never experienced with a man. She bit her lip so that anyone who was nearby wouldn't hear, but that didn't diminish the thrill that at any second they might be caught. She'd never been so reckless or wanton. Garrett brought that out in her.

Willa's breathing was heavy as she shamelessly rocked against him, soaking up every amount of pleasure he cared to give her. "I'm coming," she told him, unable to focus on anything but how he was making her feel. She buried her mouth in his shoulder and cried out, tensed and shattered in his arms before settling against him. He kissed her temple, and when she shifted, he let her down. She stood before him on shaky legs. They were both still dressed, and it was still somehow one of the most erotic moments of her life. She adjusted her clothing, part of her wishing he'd just ripped the clothes straight from her body.

Then she'd have to return to her meeting with Cathy half naked. With a moan, she pushed on Garrett's chest. She had to get back to Cathy.

Garrett was reaching for her again. "Why don't you let me take you back to my place? We can do that the proper way."

"Garrett, wait," she said as she struggled to catch her breath.

"Everything okay?"

Nothing was okay. In just a few moments of weakness, she'd completely forgotten about her vow to keep whatever was between them platonic and businesslike. "Yeah, I'm fine," she lied. "That was—"

"Intense."

She couldn't believe she was about to say this. "Yeah, and it shouldn't happen again."

"No?"

"We've talked about this," Willa told him. "It's too complicated. We can kiss and touch when we're in front of people, to keep up the charade, but when we're alone, we have to keep it to ourselves. I'm afraid of blurring the lines between the fake relationship and our friendship, and whatever our hormones are telling us to do."

He took a step back. "You're right. This is too important to screw up." He raised his hands. "I'm sorry."

"I am too."

"Willa?" Cathy called from a short distance away. She was close, and Willa had no idea if the woman had heard her as she'd cried out at Garrett's touch.

"I'm coming," she called back, unintentionally using a phrase she had just uttered in Garrett's arms.

"You sure did," he said with a grin.

"Oh, shut it, you," she said, playfully, glad that, no matter what had happened, Garrett was still her friend and that there were no hard feelings. She took one final look at him and then went off to find Cathy.

Eleven

"It's nice to see you two spending so much time together," Elias said from across the table at the restaurant.

Garrett nodded and draped his arm over Willa's chair. "We try. It's tough with her living in High Pine."

Elias turned his attention to Willa. "Have you thought about moving back home?" He had a twinkle in his eye. "Especially if things are getting serious between you."

Willa's mouth dropped open, and she looked to Garrett for guidance. He put his hand over hers. "Elias, what's with all the questions? I thought we were just having a nice dinner together."

"That doesn't mean I'm not interested in my

grandson's life. I'm just wondering how serious this has gotten. Maybe you're already close to getting married. I don't know."

Garrett bit back the annoyance he felt and tried his best to level his voice. "We're not discussing marriage yet. It's too soon for that. Right now, we're getting to know each other."

Willa nodded and put her hand on his thigh in a supportive gesture. But a frisson of electricity shot directly to his groin. Thankfully, the long white tablecloth covered his lap, and she couldn't see the impact her touch had had on him.

"I, for one, am pleased to see the two of you together. Garrett, you couldn't have found a better woman than Willa. She's sweet, kind, attentive—but I know she's tough," Cathy said.

"Yeah, I know." He smiled down at her, and he knew that the attention embarrassed her a little. "She is all of those things."

"You're not so bad yourself," she told him. "I know that you might be suspicious, Elias," she said, turning her attention to his grandfather. "We reconnected right after your announcement, and we just went from there. But I think it was just fate. We enjoy each other's company, and it just feels right."

"Couldn't have said it any better myself," Garrett said, drawing his fingertips down her cheek, capturing her attention. "It *was* like fate." Their eyes connected, and he knew that the want and need in her eyes was reflected in his.

The waiter chose that moment to arrive with their

entrées, and it broke the connection with Willa. He cleared his throat and drank some water. He thought of the last time he'd touched her. His hands traveling up and down her back before he'd lifted and pinned her to the side of the shed. It was a regrettable moment for him—not because he shouldn't have kissed her or touched her, especially when she'd been so adamant that they keep their hands to themselves; but because she deserved better than a quick grope and an orgasm on the side of a storage shed.

But since that day earlier in the week, he'd been consumed by the thought of getting her in his bed, even though they'd agreed to not let their hormones call the shots. After dinner, she'd be coming home with him—even though she would be in his guest room. He wasn't sure how he'd be able to concentrate on anything knowing that she was under his roof and he couldn't touch her.

Willa was quiet on the drive to Garrett's house. All week, she hadn't been able to think of anything else but the fact that she would be spending the night there. It would be next to impossible to sleep in his home, especially since he would clearly let her into his bed, even though it shouldn't happen. If he wasn't going to respect the rules they'd put in place, she would have to be the responsible one here and pump the brakes before they went too far.

The truck turned up the gravel road and passed the sign for Hardwell Ranch. Her heartbeat sped up in her chest, and she wondered if Garrett had clocked the deep breaths she'd been taking to steady it. They drove past the main ranch house and continued a short distance to Garrett's.

It was built in a similar style to the main house, but it wasn't quite as large. Garrett turned off the truck and unbuckled his seat belt. "Wait right there," he told her. He grabbed the small duffel she'd packed from the back and opened the passenger door. He helped her down from the high cab, and she slid her body against his as she climbed down.

She pushed open the door and immediately felt welcome as she entered Garrett's home. She'd been inside the house before, but it always amazed her. The main floor was open concept—large but still cozy, modern but rustic. The space was accented with wooden walls and an immense, stone fireplace that took up most of the wall to her right. The ceiling opened up to the top floor, making it extremely high. The kitchen was big, bright, clean and spacious, with stainless steel appliances. And despite its modern appearance and functionality, it still had all the feel of a country kitchen.

"I've been here before, but I can't believe people live like this," she said. He tapped the screen on his phone several times, and the panels on the wall moved, revealing floor-to-ceiling windows that provided an unobstructed view to the back of the house. It was similar to the same feature of the main house, of the patio and hot tub. It was dark now, but she knew that in the daylight, the house had a similar view to the main house, the sprawling ranch and mountains in the distance. In the daylight, she would surely be able to see the grassy fields of the ranch, the gentle rolling hills and trees that seemed to go on forever. There was a telescope pointed out and upward. "I can't wait to see the view in the morning."

"The night's all right too. That thing really comes in handy," he said, pointing at the telescope.

"I never took you for a stargazer."

He shrugged. "I dabble."

"Same."

A silence fell over them as they watched each other from across the room. They were both acutely aware that this was the first time they'd been alone since earlier that week. She thought of the night they'd kissed in the limo, their near miss the night of the barbecue and the way he'd brought her to orgasm outside of a storage shed. Each of those encounters had threatened to go further, but each time, they'd been interrupted before they could. But with the two of them spending the night under one roof, who would interrupt them now?

Garrett cleared his throat roughly. "Well," he said, "come see the upstairs. I'll show you the guest room."

Willa followed him up the steps. She'd never been upstairs. On the second floor, she looked over the railing to see the living room. He stopped in front of a closed door. "This is my room." He gestured to the one next to it. "And this is where you'll be sleeping," he said, opening it.

She smiled. Like the rest of the house, it was tastefully appointed. It looked comfortable. A king-size bed sat in the center of the far wall, with two nightstands flanking it. Another door led to the en suite bathroom, which held a large soaker tub that put her stand-up shower stall in her High Pine apartment to shame. But what held her attention were the French doors that led to the terrace. "Will this room work for you?" he asked, coming out onto the terrace behind her.

"This will definitely work. You have an amazing place here."

"Thanks, I worked really hard to make it my own little piece of heaven."

"It was worth it," she whispered. She turned, not realizing that he was so close to her, and she brushed his chest with her own. Try as they might to keep the physical part of their non-relationship buried, it surprised her every time how little it took for them to forget themselves. One small movement, one touch, and they turned into hormonal teenagers who couldn't control themselves.

Garrett surprised her by taking a step back. "All right, then," he about grunted. "I should turn in."

"Right. That's a good idea."

He was gone and slamming his own bedroom door before she could even say good-night.

Twelve

Garrett rolled over in bed. How was he supposed to sleep when he knew that Willa was sleeping in the bed on the other side of the wall? He'd used every ounce of restraint he could muster to walk away from her tonight. But she had put very clear boundaries in place. And he was going to respect them. "Enough of this," he said, throwing back the covers and pushing himself up. He needed a drink. That would relax him. He headed down the stairs and noticed that the light was on in the kitchen. He didn't think he'd left it on. When he got to the main floor, he saw that Willa was sitting at the kitchen table.

She turned her head and saw him. "Sorry if I woke you," she said.

"You didn't at all," he assured her. "Can't sleep?"

"Not really," she told him. "I've just got a lot on my mind. How about you?"

"The same. I think it's probably a little different having someone else here under my roof." He didn't tell her that it was because of her that he couldn't manage to get any sleep. Hell, he couldn't even close his eyes without picturing her in his arms and in his bed.

"Thanks for your hospitality," she said, as if he was the one doing her a huge favor and not the other way around.

"I hope the room is comfortable." He hated the awkwardness of the conversation. They were friends. He knew that the over-the-top politeness was just a way to put distance between them and the obvious attraction they felt for one another.

"It's great. It's just the strange bed. A different house."

Garrett went to a nearby cupboard, opened it, and reached in and pulled out a bottle of bourbon. "Want a drink? Help you sleep?"

"Yeah, that'd be great. Thanks."

He took down a couple of short glasses. He poured her a finger of bourbon and handed it to her, their fingertips touching as she accepted it. Their eyes connected, and a flare of awareness flickered briefly between them before he rounded the other side of the table, using the heavy oak as a barrier instead of taking the seat next to hers.

They sipped their drinks in silence for a moment before Willa laughed.

"What's so funny?"

"It's just so surreal. I never imagined we'd end up here."

He laughed too. "Yeah. Tell me about it. You took a little convincing, and now we're even closer to pulling this off."

He reached across the table, extending his glass to her. They clinked their glasses. "Imagine, Applewood's most notorious bachelor," Willa started, "settling down with a woman."

"Especially with the infamous 'runaway bride.'"

He'd meant it as a joke, but he knew he'd messed up when the frown formed on her face. "Damn, I'm sorry, Willa. I shouldn't have said that."

Willa held her glass so it obscured most of her face. "It's fine," she told him. "I can take it. I've heard a lot worse."

"You shouldn't have to take it from me. Especially from me. I'm your friend. I've heard some of the things that people said about you. It wasn't right. I'm sure there's a story behind what happened that day, and I'm not going to ask you to tell me unless you want to share. You must have had a good reason to run out of the wedding."

She nodded. "I did. But I admittedly waited until the last possible moment to do it." She lifted her glass and downed the bourbon. "You know, I don't really want to talk about that right now. Do you?"

"Not really." In fact, the last thing he wanted to do while shirtless in his kitchen with a pajama-clad

Willa was talk about Thomas. "As long as we're both still up, what do you want to talk about?"

"How about we talk about you? Why don't we talk about how you're dealing with all of this?"

"All of what?"

She gestured between them. "This. Us. It's been a couple of weeks, but we've never had the chance to talk about this. This is actually one of the few quiet moments we've had alone, without an audience. Elias's demands, the fake relationship. This has to be a lot for you. How are you taking it?"

"I'm fine."

"You're just *fine*? This is a lot for me. It must be even more intense for you. There's so much at stake."

"I'll be honest, it is a lot of change. But I'm keeping my mind focused on the fact that the ranch will be mine when this is all over."

"And that's all you want?"

"It's all I ever wanted," he told her. "Since I was a kid, I spent all my free time here with Elias, learning the ropes. Doing the grunt work. And then thinking about it all being taken away from me because I fail to comply with my grandfather's demands—no matter how ridiculous they are—it kills me." He drank from his glass, emptying it of bourbon. He'd never revealed that much to anyone else. He'd never told anyone how it felt to have Elias threaten his position on the ranch.

"Did it bother you, what Elias said?"

"It bothers me that he's interfering in my life," he revealed. "It also bothers me that he thinks I can't be happy if I don't settle down and find someone to love. I don't need to tell you that there's more to life than love and marriage." He chuckled to himself. The words he'd said were the complete opposite of what most people claimed. But to him, the ranch, the animals, the people—they were everything to him. He'd never considered a wife or family a priority, but as he looked at Willa on the opposite side of the table, the idea seemed damn appealing.

She poured them each other shot of bourbon and held up her glass. "I'll drink to that." Garrett joined her in the toast, and they drank. "So, what is it? Why have you never been married? You're no stranger to female company. You're a catch, and lots of women would gladly be your girlfriend. You've got no desire to settle down with one of them, get married, start a family?"

He shrugged. He hadn't been expecting to reveal his inner workings and soul to Willa, but she brought it out in him. She was so damn easy to talk to. "I'm not opposed to settling down. It was just never a priority to me. I spend so many hours a day on the ranch. Not many women can deal with the up-with-the-sun grinding all day and then collapsing into bed—I wouldn't expect anyone else to put up with that kind of life. Sure, I know how to cut loose and have fun. I'm getting better at that work-life balance. But ranching is a twenty-four-hour commitment, seven days a week. Not everyone can put up with the hours I work, and I wouldn't expect them to. So, I just figured why bother dragging someone into that life. Any energy that could go into a relationship goes into the ranch. The people, the animals—all of them depend on me. It might not be the traditional ideal, but that's family to me."

He looked back to Willa, and she was gorgeous in the glow cast from the small light over the stove top. It cast a golden glow on the left side of her face. Her hair was pinned back, but loose tendrils hung and twirled around her face. She looked at him with softness and compassion, as if she understood what he was saying. "I respect that. And I think that's why this arrangement works for me as well. I'm not about to let another man undervalue me, or not make me a priority, or not give me one hundred percent of himself."

Garrett nodded sadly. The killer of it all was, if he looked ahead, he could see a future with Willa. Yet as he thought about the life he'd built and the reasons he'd come up with, he wished they weren't true. But he couldn't put her through that. The ranch would always be his priority, especially when it was under his control. Between being out on the ranch and in the boardroom, his work hours would just extend later and later into the day. And that was why he'd never felt the need to settle down. She'd told him herself that she wouldn't put up with not being a priority, and he couldn't blame her for a second. As attracted to her as he was, he and Willa just wouldn't work.

A silence fell over them. Willa looked around—at the walls, the ceiling, the clock on the wall, anywhere but at Garrett. He'd come down shirtless, wearing only a pair of low-slung gray sweatpants. He hadn't known she was down there, sitting alone, and seeing the way he looked half-dressed, with his hair tousled by his pillow, was almost enough to make her run back up to her bedroom before she jumped on top of him. She'd known that staying in his house would be difficult; it was so hard to resist him. She wanted him, but she couldn't let herself fall for him. He'd already told her that he wouldn't put a woman before the ranch. She'd promised herself that she would not settle for anything less.

Garrett yawned and it caught her attention. "I think it's time for me to turn in."

"Early to bed, early to rise?" she asked, gathering their glasses.

They both checked the time on the wall clock. It was past midnight. "Yeah, except it's a little late for the *early to bed* part."

"Well, I guess we'd better get back up there," she said. Her own words made her pause and think about the possibility of them going back upstairs together. Except that she would be returning to her bedroom and he to his.

They both headed up the stairs and stopped in the space between his master and her guest room. She glanced into his room and at the rumpled sheets on his king-size bed, the ones he'd tousled, unable to fall asleep, just like her. She wondered if he'd been thinking about her, just as she'd been thinking about him.

"Good night, Willa," he said, but they both stayed

in place, even though her head was screaming at her to get in her room and shut the door. She couldn't make her legs move to step away from him. Instead, she leaned against the wall and looked up at him, and sighed in resignation. When it came to Garrett, especially since he was half naked in front of her, she couldn't resist him.

She gave up trying.

"You know, I've been thinking a lot about that day."

He narrowed his eyes and grinned. "Which day? This week?"

"Yeah," she said. "It was incredible."

"I know, but you deserve better than to be pinned against a shed."

"Remember when we agreed to not let things get physical between us? We wanted to stop it from getting complicated?"

"Yeah."

She took a step closer. "I think we're failing at that."

"Willa…" His voice held a hint of warning.

"Yes?"

"What are we doing here?"

She didn't answer him but instead, leaned in and kissed him. He pulled her close, and his mouth took hers. He dragged her into his room. Their hands were everywhere. She ran her fingers over his torso, marveling at the tanned skin and well-formed muscles underneath. She ran her fingers over the soft hair that covered his chest. His fingers toyed with the

bottom hem of her tank top. She willed him to re-
move it, and he obliged, leaving her topless. They
were skin-to-skin, and she knew that there would
be no going back.

Garrett turned on the lamp by the bed. If he was
going to be with Willa, he was going to be able to
see every inch of her. He went to her, and he kissed
her again, stoking the fires deep within both of them
with his lips and his tongue. He put his hands on
her waist and smoothed them upward, finding her
breasts.

He kissed her once again and walked her to the
wall behind her, pressing her against it. He kissed her
neck, striking every sensitive spot along her throat,
stopping at the crook where her neck met her shoulder. She smoothed her hands over the bare skin of his
back, and she pulled him closer. He ventured lower,
kissing his way down her chest, pausing to pay some
attention to her breasts, taking her nipples between his
lips and playing with them until they were tight, rigid
bumps, before lowering further until he was kneel-
ing in front of her. His hands cupped her hips, and
then he lowered her shorts. Garrett looked up at her;
Willa's eyes were hot with desire, and her bottom lip
was caught between her teeth. He raised his eyebrows
in question, and she quickly nodded. He let go of the
breath he'd been holding and leaned in to sample the
neat triangle of trimmed hair at the apex of her thighs,
opening his mouth over her.

Garrett grasped her ankle and put her leg over his

shoulder, and he moved in. He used his fingers to part her folds, and with one long swipe of his tongue, he tasted her. She was like honey in his mouth—sweet, warm—and he went back for another taste.

Willa threw her head against the wall behind her. Garrett's mouth on her was incredible. His tongue slid lazily over her while his fingers entered her, withdrew and delved into her again. As his tongue continued to lash against the sensitive ball of nerves, she couldn't stop the lustful cry that rose in her throat.

Willa's pulse thundered, and her breathing quickened as the waves of pleasure radiated from her center. She was standing on one leg, her other thrown over Garrett's shoulder, and when she almost fell, she reached down and grasped his hair and shoulder. He grabbed her hips, holding her to him as he stayed with her while her orgasm tore through her body. Uncontrollably, she fisted his hair, and she knew she was pulling, but she couldn't help it. He was doling out such sweet pleasure that she wasn't cognizant of anything else around her.

When she quieted, Garrett stood before her, and he kissed her deeply. She could taste herself on his lips and in his mouth, She wrapped her arms around his neck and pulled him closer, kissing him as fervently as he was kissing her. Without breaking apart, Garrett lifted her and walked her to the bed, then gently lowered her onto the center of the mattress.

He kneeled on the mattress, between her spread

thighs, and he looked down at her, his gaze burning a trail over her. Willa, however, was transfixed by his body. His well-sculpted pecs and ridged abdominals that were dusted with hair.

Willa needed him, but when she reached out for him, Garrett backed away slightly. He reached into his bedside table, and pulled out a condom.

He rolled the latex over his length, and Willa held her breath impatiently as he kneeled above her, and then he was inside her in one thrust.

She cried out, feeling him as he filled her. He was still, perhaps taking a moment as well. But Willa was impatient. She began thrusting her hips toward him, using him to chase her own pleasure. Soon, Garrett snapped out of his trance and began moving himself. But he set the pace. He held down her hips and moved slowly, in and out of her. Pulling himself most of the way out before pushing into her again as far as he could go. The slow pace was replaced by harder, more forceful thrusts from him, and with every one, he brought her to newer heights.

Willa felt her second orgasm of the night take her over, and she couldn't wait; she shifted so that she could be an equal partner, so that she could meet his hips. They both became frantic—hands grabbing at the other, their kisses sloppy, their breaths mingling—until she cried out his name as a powerful rush tore through her.

Nothing and no one existed but them and their own pleasure. When her breathing slowed, Garrett continued to thrust his hips, pumping into her, until he stilled and murmured her name, a rough whisper in her ear.

When he rolled back to her, he put his arms around her and scooped her close. "Damn, Willa," he whispered into her hair. "That was good. I don't know why we've been denying ourselves all this time."

She hummed her satisfaction as she drew circles in his chest hair. "I know." The peal of his cell phone filled his bedroom. They separated, quickly, as if they'd been caught. Both regarded the other with matching dazed looks. They'd had another indiscretion. But Willa didn't think it would be the last. He reached for the phone. It was past midnight. Whoever was on the other end would be calling for a reason.

"Hello?"

Willa watched as Garrett listened to whatever he was being told. His demeanor changed as he took it in. His jaw was hard, and his eyes focused, but she could see the worry there. "Okay, I'll be right there." He hung up.

"Who was that? What's wrong?"

"It was Dylan. One of the horses is giving birth. She's doing okay, but I need to get out there."

"Want me to come with?"

"No," Garrett said, pushing away from her and out of bed. She missed his warmth and quickly pulled her pajamas back on. He dressed just as quickly, and she was left alone in his bedroom.

Walking into his guest room, she looked out the window and saw him ride off on an ATV. She shouldn't be disappointed that he'd left. But she couldn't beat the frown that formed on her lips. She knew that he wanted to be there for the birth of the foal. He'd explicitly told her that the ranch was the most important thing to him, and she would never come first with him. Despite how good they were together—physically, sexually—it hit home that she would never be his priority. They would never work as a couple.

She turned on the shower and realized that this was exactly what she was afraid of happening. She'd somehow allowed herself to fall for Garrett, and she knew that he would just break her heart.

When Garrett arrived at the stable on his ATV, he tried to force what had happened with Willa out of his mind. This was the kind of thing he'd been talking about. Ranching was a 24/7 job. It wasn't fair that he'd left Willa in his house so he could deal with an animal's health. He couldn't expect any woman to put up with that. Dylan exited the stable.

"Daisy's on her way," he told him.

They didn't always call in the vet for livestock births, but the horse had shown complications during the gestation.

"Good. How is she?"

"One of the ranch hands on night watch heard the noise and went to check it out. She was in labor, and he called me."

"Thanks for letting me know."

"Sorry I woke you up."

"It's okay. I wasn't asleep."

"Did I see Willa's car in the driveway?"

"Yeah."

Dylan's jaw hardened at the implication that Willa was the reason Garrett hadn't been sleeping. He might be okay with Garrett and Willa in a relationship, but he certainly wouldn't want any of the details. But they both knew there were more important things to worry about. Garrett went into the stable to check on the mare. He put a supportive hand on the horse, knowing that she was stressed and in pain. He wanted to comfort her.

"Daisy's here," Dylan called.

"Good. She's going to help you out there, girl. Don't worry." He cleared out of the way to give Daisy and her assistant room to work.

He stepped back outside with Dylan, making sure they weren't in the way of the birth. Dylan was quiet, and Garrett was grateful. It gave him a chance to think about Willa. He'd seen the look on her face when he'd gotten out of bed. Maybe he should have explained it to her a little more how important some ranch duties were—a new birth being one of the most important ones. But he didn't think that would have helped. He didn't want to hurt her—that was the last thing he wanted to do. The problem was with him. He would have to figure out a way to care for the ranch but also foster relationships, including this apparently fake one. He just wasn't sure how to do that.

The next morning, when Garrett awoke, he immediately smelled coffee, and he groaned in anticipation. It had been after sunrise by the time the foal had received a quick checkup by Daisy, and he and Dylan were finally able to return to their homes. It had been a long night, but he was grateful to have been there and see the newest addition to the herd being born.

But during the long, dark night, Willa hadn't been far from his mind. He knew he'd goofed up by leaving his bed immediately, not having bothered to check on her. He was used to the bachelor life, coming and going—*quite literally*—as he pleased. But with another person in his life, whether she was a fake girlfriend or not, she deserved some consideration.

He heard her in the kitchen. It sounded like she was making breakfast, so he pushed himself out of bed and headed downstairs.

"Mornin'," he said to her back as she stood at the stove.

"Mornin'," she called back without turning to face him. Was she pissed at him? Probably. He poured himself a cup of coffee, watching her as she whisked scrambled eggs. "How's the foal?" she finally asked.

"Everything is fine. You should head down there later. She's pretty cute."

"Maybe I will."

"Are we okay?"

"We're fine."

"I just might be a clueless man, but it doesn't feel like we are." She said nothing. "Last night—" he started.

"Was a mistake," she completed.

"That's not what I was going to say," he told her.

"But it's true." She turned to face him. "When you left last night, I was disappointed. Not in you," she clarified. "In myself. I thought I could do this," she told him. "It's why we should have kept things platonic. I was wrong, coming on to you last night."

"It didn't feel wrong."

"No, it was incredible. And that's the problem. I'm afraid that I'm just going to keep wanting more and more of you. And you can't give me that."

He stayed silent. Willa was laying everything out, and he couldn't deny it. Hell, he'd left her arms for ranch duties the night before. He couldn't tell her it wouldn't happen again. And that wasn't fair to her. "You're right."

"I feel like I should go." She went to move past him, but he reached out and took her hand, stopping her.

"No, wait," he told her. "Is our arrangement still on?" he asked.

"I told you I would do it, Garrett. I'm a woman of my word. I just need some space."

"Maybe it's best if we speed up the timeline," he suggested.

"What do you mean?"

"You move in here, and we get engaged, have the wedding sooner, rather than later, and then we're done."

She nodded. "Maybe that's a good idea. The quicker we can get this done, the better."

Thirteen

A few weeks later, Willa drove into Applewood, but this time, the trunk of her car was packed with everything she would need to officially "move" into Garrett's ranch house.

When Garrett had suggested the move, even though she'd known it was coming, it filled her with dread. Her apartment in High Pine was the first space she'd ever had that was her own, and now she was moving into the home of yet another man.

She'd been out of college less than a year before she'd met Thomas, and he'd wined and dined her, asking her to move in with him soon thereafter. He'd had charm, charisma, wealth, and she'd never experienced anything like it before. He'd moved her in and then showed her what a monster he was. He wouldn't let her have her own friends; he wouldn't let her work. He didn't even want her seeing her brother. But she was beholden to him. She had no job, no money of her own. Dylan hadn't wanted her to marry Thomas, and she didn't want to run crying to him. As a child, she'd only wanted a home of her own, and she'd had one, but it had come at a spectacular price.

She frowned at the memories and turned on the radio. A country song played. A woman singing about not needing any man to complete her life. Willa blew out a frustrated breath. That was how she had wanted to live. After Thomas, she'd promised herself she would never rely on a man for money or possessions again. But here she was, turning up the driveway to Hardwell Ranch, with her bags packed to move into Garrett Hardwell's guest bedroom.

She and Garrett had kept each other at arm's length for weeks, and she was unsure how this move would go. They could pretend to be a loving couple in front of everyone, but in private, they now avoided one another. She hadn't expected it, but the lying was wearing on her. She could tell herself that what she was doing was helping Garrett—and herself— but when friends and family shared how happy they were for the couple, it felt like a gut punch.

When she arrived in front of his house, he was already standing outside on the wraparound porch. He was wearing his jeans and a button-down shirt and a black cowboy hat, his thumbs hooked around his belt loops. He smiled at her as she exited her car.

"You made it," he said, walking toward her with an easy gait. "I was afraid you were gonna chicken out," he joked, greeting her with a hug. She felt both of them pause in the embrace, as if deciding if they should take it further. But thankfully, he released her before walking around her Mini to the hatchback. She popped the trunk door, and he pulled out her suitcase. That and the duffel in the back seat were all she'd brought. She left as much as she could at her High Pine apartment, just to maintain that tie to the place and her independence.

Garrett stepped aside so she could walk into the house first, and when they climbed the stairs with her things, he surprised her by bringing her suitcase into his room while she waited in the doorway of the guest room. "What are you doing?"

"I'm bringing in your suitcase so you can unpack. I made room in my closet."

"Why do you think I'm sleeping in here?"

"Because it would seem awful curious to anyone who came by if all of your things were in the guest room."

He was right, of course; she just hadn't realized that they would be sharing a bed. That would surely be the first test.

"Listen," he said, his hands up, resigned. "I'll sleep in the guest room. We just have to make it look like you live here. That's all I care about."

That's all I care about. The phrase ran through her head and was a good reminder that she shouldn't let her hormones get the better of her again. It firmed her resolve to remember what the arrangement was. "It's fine," she told him. "We'll both sleep in here." If she just remembered why she was doing this—to help Garrett get the ranch, and for her to finally take possession of her family's property—she would have no trouble keeping her hands to herself.

"You're sure?"

"Yes, of course. We're both adults. We should be able to sleep in the same bed without losing control, don't you think?"

The look he gave her was dangerous to her resolve. "If you say so."

Later that night, Garrett waited in his en suite bathroom until he heard Willa get into bed. Their first night in the house together since their disagreement had gone better than he'd thought it would. They'd shared a nice dinner, sat on the patio and just watched the sky, pointing out constellations and shooting stars. They'd even watched a couple of movies. As if they'd both been putting off the time when they would have to crawl into the same bed together.

On the other side of the door, his bedroom was silent, and in the lamplight, he saw that Willa was already in bed, curled into a ball on his side of the bed. She was so still that he knew there was no way she was already asleep. They had to go to sleep, so he might as well not prolong it.

He walked to the other side of the bed, then lifted the sheets and slid between them. He had a king-size mattress, but he was still aware that Willa was on the other side of it. He could feel her warmth, smell her shampoo, and he grew hard, remembering the last time he'd had her in his bed.

He closed his eyes and turned to face away from her. But he knew that sleep wouldn't come. He was so racked with desire that he could barely move, barely breathe, lest his resolve to not touch her completely crumble.

That's why he was surprised when she said his name. "Garrett," she whispered in the darkness. "Are you asleep?"

"No," he muttered, his body as taut as a wire.

"I can't sleep."

"Neither can I."

She took a deep, shaky breath, and he knew that she was as needy as he was. "What do you suppose we do about it?"

Willa was still facing away from Garrett, but she felt him roll over in the bed. He came closer, pressing himself against her back. She could feel how much he wanted her too. She turned around in his arms so they were chest to chest. She stretched her neck and placed a simple kiss on his lips.

That was all the permission he needed. Like every one of their touches and kisses before it, this one led to more. He rolled so that he was lying over her, then took her mouth in another kiss. Her hands made their way underneath the hem of his T-shirt, and as she skimmed her fingertips along the ridges of his abdominal muscles, she pushed his shirt up and over his head. That was his signal. He deepened the kiss and pulled her own shirt over her head. He pressed his weight against her, being careful not to crush her. He was strong, powerful and in a dominant position, but Willa knew that she was in control, behind the wheel, and she was determined to let him know where they were going.

They'd started the night with awkward conversation over dinner, but they'd managed to turn it around, convincing themselves that they could be friendly without losing control. She should have known it was a lie. She'd tried to convince herself that she didn't need his touch, but as he explored her skin with his lips and fingertips, she knew it was a damn lie.

Balancing his weight on one elbow, Garrett cupped her breasts with his large hands before he kissed his way down her throat, over her chest.

He kissed his way to her nipple, where he sucked and nipped at her. Willa arched her back, pushing closer against him. Stopping only to take a condom from the bedside table and roll it on, he settled between her thighs and pushed inside her. His thrusts were long, slow, and she savored every bit of them.

Their moans filled the room, mingling and growing into a crescendo as Willa cried out, pushing against Garrett as he plunged into her one final time, growling out his completed satisfaction in her ear.

His head dropped to her shoulder. Her skin was electrified by his kiss as he lit her nerve endings on fire. She squirmed involuntarily with the feeling and giggled as his mouth tickled her.

He raised his head and looked down at her. His smile was wide and satisfied. His hair fell over his forehead, and Willa pushed it back. He kissed her again, his tongue snaking into her mouth quickly before retreating. He rolled off her and discreetly disposed of the condom before he scooped her back into his arms, pulling her across his chest.

She twirled a finger in the curly hair on his chest and then flattened her palms over his sternum. Resting her chin on her hands, she smiled at him. "That was great."

"I was afraid you were going to tell me it was a mistake again."

She shook her head. "No, I don't know how we thought we'd be able to keep ourselves from doing it again. Maybe it was just a onetime thing, you know—get it out of our systems."

"You're joking," he replied, trailing his fingers up and down her spine, causing her to shiver. "I don't know where we're going with this, but I know we can't resist each other. So why fight it? Why deny ourselves this pleasure for as long as we have each other?" She didn't say anything. "Tell me I'm wrong."

"I can't. Life is short. Which is why we need to get through this relationship and get married and get on with our lives." She felt a pang of sadness at the finality.

"YOLO, right?" he joked.

* * *

"How do you think our charade is going so far?" she asked, filling the silence after several moments.

"I think we're doing a great job."

"Me too. Especially if they could see us like this," she said, catching their reflection in his full-length mirror. "We definitely look like a functional couple."

"Well, I hope they don't see us like this," Garrett said with a laugh.

She playfully smacked his chest. "You know what I mean."

"I do. I wonder if it's time to take it to the next level."

He felt her stiffen in his arms, and she looked up at him. "What do you mean?"

"My family is already convinced that we're a great couple. Do you think we should announce our engagement?" She exhaled, her breath cool against his skin. "Are you okay?"

"Yeah, I'm fine. It's just that it's the beginning of the biggest step, isn't it? The marriage is an intense proposition. It's going to get a lot more complicated from here. It's all well and good to say we're dating and living together, but we'll be lying to your family about something as big as a marriage."

"Have you changed your mind about all of this?" Garrett tensed, awaiting her answer.

"No, I haven't changed my mind. I told you I'd do this, so I will. It's just going to be hard to keep up the charade."

"I know, but we can just end this if you want. I

don't want you to feel bad every time we see our friends and family." The thing was, he didn't want it to end. She was quickly becoming the best part of his life. Maybe Elias had been onto something. Maybe there was something to having a partner, someone to share your life with.

"No, it'll be fine. I want to help you do this."

"Do you have any plans next weekend?" he asked.

"No," she said, shifting closer to him. "Why do you ask?"

"I think we should invite the family over for dinner. Would you like that?"

"Yeah, that sounds like fun."

He put his arm around her waist and drew her closer. He loved the way she felt pressed against him. His body was already reacting to her again. "We can show them what a great couple we are."

"Sounds great."

"Thanks. I'll get a ring tomorrow. Do you have any requests?"

"There's no need to go through with getting a new ring. I could just use Thomas's."

Garrett bristled. "You still have it?"

"It's in my apartment somewhere. I held on to it when I moved, in case I needed the cash or something when I first left. He never asked for it back."

He picked up her hand and brought it to his mouth, kissing her ring finger. "There's no way I'm going to let you wear another man's ring when you're engaged to me—whether it's real or not."

* * *

Whether it's real or not. The moment they'd shared—it was too much for her. This was supposed to be a fake relationship. She was doing it for money, and at worst, she'd hoped for a quick romp in the hay. It wasn't supposed to get any deeper than that. She wasn't supposed to catch...*feelings.* But she could no longer deny it. She was in love with Garrett.

Garrett's gaze on her and the way he touched her—with such careful attention—it made her ache. She wanted him so much, and she'd gotten him. She was going to marry him, but it would mean nothing. Her heart stuttered in her chest. *Don't be stupid*, she told herself. Garrett had explained to her what marriage with him would be like. He'd described to her a life in which he would be too busy to show her a real relationship. It wasn't what she wanted out of life. She'd vowed to never let herself be with a man who didn't treat her like a priority in their relationship.

Whether it's real or not. No matter how she felt, those words—especially the "or not" part—hit her square in the stomach, as they explained what Garrett's feelings were about their arrangement. They might be getting closer, but she was still going to be his fake wife, and once they both got what they wanted, they would cut ties and part ways.

Willa felt her eyes fill with frustrated tears. She had to get away before Garrett noticed.

"Hey," he said, cupping her cheek. *Too late.* He'd noticed. "Are you okay?"

"I'm fine," she said, shaking herself free of her

emotions and his touch. "We should really get some sleep. We both have to work tomorrow."

"Talk to me. There's something wrong. If you think we should end it or if there's anything else that has to do with me, tell me. Are you not okay with our arrangement?" he asked, "because if you aren't, I need to know."

Her eyes widened. It reminded her that even though they'd shared an amazing night, Garrett had still brought her in as part of an arrangement. It wasn't a real relationship and they were both doing it for money. "No, I'm fine," she told him.

As Willa lay next to him sleeping, Garrett found himself staring at the ceiling. Dammit, they'd had an incredible night they'd just shared. He still had no idea what he'd said to make her push away from him. They had been enjoying the moment and each other, and then the mood had shifted in only a matter of seconds.

He didn't know how to draw her out. He wasn't used to talking about feelings or being emotionally open to someone. He had no idea how to even ask. It was late, and he needed to sleep. As always, he had to get an early start on the ranch, but at the moment, he didn't care. His brain, his life, his heart had become consumed with Willa.

Tomorrow he would go out and buy her an engagement ring. It was the next step in their fake relationship. Garrett had never wanted to be married—the ranch consumed his life—but when it came to Willa, he'd be damned if he didn't wish what they had was real. He reached out and touched her cheek. But he'd never do that to her. Being with a man who was occupied by something else was not what she wanted, and it wasn't what she deserved.

He knew he was falling in love with Willa, but he knew they couldn't have a future together. He would just have to settle with what he could get from their current relationship—whether it was real, or not.

Fourteen

After another near-sleepless night, Garrett made his way across the ranch to the bunkhouse, where some of the ranch hands were hanging out. Dylan was already there, along with some people he didn't recognize.

"I went ahead and hired the new ranch hands," Dylan explained quietly, off to the side.

"Already?"

"It had to be done to train in time for fall. We talked about this."

"Yeah, I know. I've just been distracted lately. Sorry."

"Yeah, you have a lot going on."

It irritated Garrett that there were things going on with the ranch that he didn't know about, as his mind, heart and life had become consumed with Willa. But he trusted Dylan and all his guys to take care of the place when he couldn't focus on it one hundred percent.

He introduced himself to the new hires. "How's your day looking, guys?" he said, addressing them all. They knew their next boss was in front of them, so all the ranch hands—even ones whom he'd worked with side by side for years—stood a little straighter, more attentive. He didn't like this shift in attitude. He might be in charge of the ranch very soon, but he didn't want his crew to treat him any differently.

He still felt that he was slowly losing a grasp on the day-to-day operations of the ranch. It just reaffirmed to him that a serious, committed relationship would take needed time away from his duties. He didn't want to be just a part-time rancher, even if he owned the place.

"Dylan's got us heading to the eastern edge to make sure all the cattle are corralled," Billy, one of the old-timers, answered. "Taking the new guys to show them around."

"Good. I saw a herd on the west end, too, if a couple of you want to head over that way."

"Anything else?" Billy asked.

"I need someone to make a perimeter run to make sure the fencing is all intact. There have been coyote sightings on the cameras."

"Yessir."

Garrett turned back to Dylan. "Can I talk to you in private?"

Dylan frowned. "Yeah, of course. What's up?"

He wasn't sure where he stood with Willa at the moment, but he knew the arrangement was still on, and he had to push through. "I want to ask Willa to marry me."

Dylan's eyebrows raised in an expression that Garrett wasn't sure how to read.

"What do you think about that?" he asked.

"What do you mean, what do I think? It's awesome," Dylan said, breaking into a smile and pulling Garrett in for a hug. "I just can't believe it. She's been through so much crap, and I love to see that she's happy again—and with you! I'm really happy for you."

Garrett hadn't been sure how Dylan would react, but his exuberance surprised him. But the fact that he was lying to his friend made him feel lower than a snake's belly.

Fifteen

The week passed, and things had been tense between Willa and Garrett, but they still agreed to go along with the dinner they'd planned for the family. They'd been friendly together and, in public, showed love as a couple would do; but they hadn't made love, or even slept in the same bed since the night she'd finally realized that she would never be able to have all of Garrett.

Willa walked into the kitchen, where the caterers were busy moving around. "Is there any way I can help?" Willa asked.

"Willa, darlin'," Garrett said, coming up behind her, placing a hand on her waist. "Leave the caterers alone." He handed her a glass of wine. "Come on. People are arriving." Together, they walked into the family room, and she saw that Cathy, Elias and Garrett's parents were there. And of course, Dylan.

Garrett had planned the family dinner, and while she was happy to see the people he'd gathered, things just hadn't been the same between them since their conversation the other night. While they were still cordial to one another, they were reserving their "couple behavior" for when people were around. Together, they greeted their guests. She'd never grown up having large family functions. She was starting to appreciate having so many friends and family around.

Garrett picked up a fork and tapped it against his whiskey glass, gaining the attention of everyone gathered. "Thank you all for coming tonight. With everyone being so busy, and Elias and Cathy planning their wedding and move, it's been a while since we all got together." He reached for Willa and pulled her to his side. "We all gathered here recently for Elias and Cathy's engagement party, where Elias announced his retirement and really gave me a come-to-Jesus moment." Willa cautioned a look at Elias, who was watching both of them carefully. But Garrett carried on, unhindered. "Through his demands, he showed me the importance of having a good, beautiful woman at my side." He raised his glass in his grandfather's direction. "You inspired me, Elias. Thank you." He looked down at Willa. "And thank you, Willa, for opening my eyes. I love you."

Willa's breath caught in her throat. Since their fight, they hadn't discussed saying the *L* word. Especially not saying it in front of everyone. The words, however, did something else to her. They made her feel light-headed. It was the first time in so long that she'd heard those words. But this time, they meant nothing. Everything—his hand on her waist, the way he looked down at her, the words themselves—was as fake as a three-dollar bill. Her throat was dry, and her tongue felt thick, but she managed to say, "I love you too," in a husky voice. She wanted to tell herself that the words were nothing, meaningless, but she couldn't. Whether she liked it—whether she'd meant it—or not, she couldn't.

The look that passed between them was intense. She wondered if the same emotions were fighting in his mind. But he was unreadable. As she looked around at the smiling, encouraging, expectant looks from the family and friends who'd gathered, she forced herself to remember that it was just a show for them. Garrett had explicitly told her how he hadn't been interested in falling in love. His feelings weren't real. He was just a good actor.

He continued on with a smile on his face. "On that note, in front of all of you here tonight, I'd like to ask Willa a very important question." Her eyes widened. Only an idiot wouldn't be able to see what was about to happen. Her breath halted in her lungs. He turned to face her. "Willa, will you marry me?" She blinked and watched him pull a small square box out of his pocket and open it. "I hope you like it."

He opened the box and showed her the most exquisite diamond ring she'd ever seen. A large diamond was flanked by three smaller diamonds on either side. "It's beautiful."

He lifted the ring from its satin bedding and slid it onto her finger. It fit perfectly. "You never answered my question, though," he prompted her. "Will you marry me?"

Before this arrangement, she'd thought that the next time she heard those words, if she ever heard them again, it would be the real thing. That she would be accepting a marriage proposal from someone she truly loved. She looked up at Garrett and realized that it was true. She was in love with him, and even though her brain knew it was dumb, her heart didn't care. She should walk away right now and save herself the future heartache. Too late. She was hook, line and sinker in love, and she knew it would destroy her. "Yes," she finally answered. "Of course I'll marry you."

The crowd around them whooped, and Garrett wrapped his arms around her and lifted her as he kissed her. When they broke apart, she looked around. Instead of seeing the curious, cynical glances she'd anticipated, Garrett's family broke out in cheers and congratulations. They were happy for them, not at all skeptical about the circumstances or the motivation surrounding their quickie engagement.

"Thank you for welcoming me into your home. I've had a great time with all of you." Willa was grateful that the Hardwells had never judged her for her past. Everyone in Applewood seemed to have their own opinions on Willa and what she'd done. But the Hardwells seemed to accept her for who she was.

"We're just glad to see Garrett so happy," Cathy told her. "He's finally learning how to let the work take a back seat and have a life."

"And now that you're getting married," Elenore, Garrett's stepmother, added. "I have to admit, I think we all thought that he was paying you to marry him because Elias was forcing him to. But seeing the two of you together, it's obvious that you're made for each other."

Willa had no response for that. These kind people all believed that she and Garrett were in love. And she was lying straight to their faces. She couldn't think of another thing to say but a weak "We're so happy together."

"And we know you've had some trouble in the past, but we can't blame you for what you did. If you aren't happy, you can't go through with it. You have to be serious about marriage, and you shouldn't fake or force it," Cathy said to her.

Even though their words were meant to be supportive, little did Cathy and the others know that she and Garrett were faking everything about their relationship. She thought back to their nights in bed, having Garrett's strong arms wrapped around her, on the softest sheets imaginable, inhaling his warm scent as she drifted off to sleep. The moment had felt so pure, sensual, loving. Maybe they weren't faking *everything*.

People hollered and embraced them—everyone except Dylan, who watched from a far corner. Their eyes connected, and she extricated herself from the huddle to go to him.

"Congratulations are in order, I guess," he said, drawing her in for a hug.

"You're happy for me?" she asked.

"Of course, I am. I never pictured you and Garrett getting together—and so fast—but I love you both, and I know you'll be happy together."

Willa tried to swallow past the lump in her throat. "Thank you," she managed to choke out. With tears in her eyes, she hugged him. How would sweet Dylan feel to know that his sister and his best friend were lying to him? What would happen when they annulled the marriage? "I love you, Dylan."

"I love you, too, Will."

She broke away from Dylan and left the room without saying anything. She nodded her thanks to a well-wisher as she crossed the room to Garrett, her husband-to-be.

"I need to talk to you."

"Yeah, sure, sweetheart," he said. "Let's go upstairs."

She followed him up the staircase, and they walked into his bedroom. Garrett shut the door partway and turned to her. "Are you okay?" he asked.

"No."

"What? You don't like the ring?"

"It's not the ring. It's beautiful. It's the proposal. I didn't know you were doing it today. It's a lot."

"I wanted to surprise you. I wanted your authentic response. As if I was really proposing. It would have been a surprise."

"Yeah, I get that. It's just that this isn't exactly the

romantic proposal of my dreams." He started to say something, but she had to stop him. "No, it's fine. I guess I just thought the next time someone gave me a ring, it would be for real, with someone I loved," she added after a beat.

"I know things have been weird between us lately, and I meant to talk to you earlier, but I thought it would be best to surprise you. But we can do it privately, if you want." Taking her hand, he slid the ring from her finger. With a smile, he got on one knee and looked up at her. "Willa Statler, will you make me the happiest man in the world by doing me the honor of being my fake wife? In sickness and health, richness and poorness, and charades and farces?"

Before he could put the ring back on her finger, she caught his hand and held the ring in her palm. "I can't marry you," she whispered. She felt the silent tears trail down her cheeks.

"What do you mean?"

"I can't do this. I can't keep lying to our friends and family. I can't be with you but not have all of you. This is a fake relationship, but it's starting to feel too real, and it kills me that it isn't."

"Willa," he said, getting up and taking a step, his arms outstretched to embrace her, but she moved out of his reach.

"No. We should have known better than to have a fake relationship and get married so you can get the ranch. I should have known better than to let that happen. The first minute the feelings got too intense,

I should have ended it there." She put the ring on the bed. "I'm sorry, Garrett, but I just can't do this."

"Well." They heard a voice at the door. It was Elias, and from the look on his face, he'd heard everything. "I should have listened to my gut. It was telling me that this whole relationship wasn't the real thing. But I wanted it to be real for you."

"Elias—" Garrett started.

The older man pointed a finger at him. "No. Let me finish. I never thought you would lie to me, let alone break the agreement that you signed." He shook his head. "The deal is off, Garrett. It's over. You'll get the same share of the ranch as your brothers and cousins will, but no more. You won't get the controlling share."

Willa gasped. She'd cost Garrett everything he'd wanted—and in turn, she wouldn't get what *she* wanted either. But that didn't matter. "Garrett," she said. "I'm sorry."

"Don't talk to me." He turned his fury on her. "This would have worked out fine if you'd just kept your end of the bargain. But I should have known this would blow up in my face. I knew I should have found someone else."

"You don't get to talk to me like that, Garrett Hardwell. This isn't my fault, and you know it. Your own dishonesty played as big a role in this. Go to hell." Without another word, she left the room. Elias followed her, and Garrett was left alone, just him and the diamond ring on the bed.

Sixteen

Willa parked her car outside of Thomas's office at the city hall. It had been a week since she'd walked out of Garrett's house. One week since she'd scuttled her life and the hopes she'd hinged her future on. She missed Garrett so much that sometimes the pain was unbearable. Thank God they hadn't gone any further with the charade. She couldn't imagine the damage that could have been done if she'd let it go on any longer. But whether Garrett was in her life or not, she could still take control of her future. And that meant seeing Thomas one more time.

Willa walked into the lobby. "Is he in?" she asked his secretary.

"The mayor is on a call," she responded.

Willa nodded but walked past the secretary's desk

and into Thomas's office. He looked shocked to see her there. "I'll have to call you back," he told whomever was on the other end. He took a deep breath and attempted to compose himself from the surprise her arrival had caused him. "Willa, you can't just barge in here."

"Looks like I just did."

"Why don't you have a seat?"

She crossed her arms and shook her head, opting to remain standing, using a power dynamic that he'd used on her and many others over the years. "I'm fine standing."

His brow furrowed. "What can I do for you, Willa?"

"You don't have to do anything, but I'm just here to tell you that I'm absolutely done being bullied by you. I'm done with caring about the rumors and the innuendo of the people in town. It stops today."

"What makes you so certain?"

"Do you remember our wedding day?"

He scoffed. "Yes. Vividly. I remember that you humiliated me in front of all of my friends and family."

"It's only fair, because you humiliated me for years." She walked over to the window and looked out on to Applewood's Main Street. The town was still small but had grown in recent years. She turned back to Thomas. "Do you want to know why I walked out?"

"Because you have a flair for the dramatic. Or maybe it's more accurate that you're a coward."

"A coward? No, Thomas, walking back up that aisle in front of everyone was the most courageous thing I've done. For so long, I'd put up with the terrible way you treated me, because that's all I thought I'd deserved." For a moment, she wavered, thinking of the way Garrett had treated her during their too-brief time together. They hadn't even been a real couple, but he'd made her feel like the most special woman in the world. She turned her attention back to her ex. "But I do deserve more."

"Is that why you're here? To tell me that you deserve more?"

"No, that's not why I'm here." She placed a check on his desk. "I want my property." The number on the check might not be the amount she needed. There was no way she was going to be able to pull that together without the money from Garrett—she could say goodbye to that—but it was a large enough amount for him to take her seriously.

"Where did you get this money? Steal it from Hardwell?"

"I didn't steal anything," she told him. She'd sold Thomas's engagement ring. Giving him back the money to buy the property seemed almost poetic. "I know it's not what you demanded, but it's a start. Sign over the property to me, and I'll keep paying you."

Thomas laughed. He still wasn't taking her seriously. "While I'm enjoying this display of backbone, Willa, I'm afraid I can't do that."

She paused. "Why not?"

"I no longer own it."

"What?"

"You heard me. I sold it. You're literally a day late, and more than a dollar short. What are you going to do now?"

She thought about that. "Nothing," she said simply. "You aren't worth it. I just want to forget you."

Willa left the check on the desk and walked out of Thomas's office, crestfallen, and got in her car. Her plan had failed. She had nothing. She didn't have her house; she didn't have her dreams. She didn't have Garrett. Her plan to stay in Applewood had been thwarted. What was her reason to stay now?

She started her car. Where would she go? She thought about High Pine, but even that area had left her with too many memories. She could go farther afield, she guessed. She could go anywhere. Back to Denver, where she'd gone to college. Las Vegas, Miami, New York City, Cincinnati—anywhere that caught her fancy. Dylan would be sad, but he would get over it. There was nothing left for her in Applewood. But first, she had one stop to make.

She pulled up in front of the property. The Sold sign was prominently displayed. The last bit of hope she'd had had left her body. Now she felt nothing for the town and what had happened to her. She was ready to leave for good. She got out of her car and saw that there was a black truck parked near the back. The current owners, no doubt. She didn't want to have to see anyone or explain why she was on their new property.

"Wait," she heard a familiar voice call to her. She turned and saw Garrett walking toward her, wearing his usual uniform of a button-down shirt, worn Levi's and a cowboy hat. He was carrying an envelope under his arm. He smiled. "I was hoping you'd show up at some point."

"What are you doing here?"

He turned back to look at the house. "I came to check out my new purchase."

"What? You bought this place?" If she hadn't been so shocked, she might have been upset.

But he smiled. "I did."

"But why?"

He shook his head. "That's a good question. Lord knows I don't need a new project right now. What am I supposed to do with this place? Fix it up and open an inn or something?"

She grinned. "That's one idea," she told him.

"That sounds like a lot of work, though. Maybe I'll just give it away."

"Who will want this dump?" she asked, playing along.

"I don't know. Hopefully, I can find someone." After a moment, he handed over the envelope. "I've got an idea. Do you want it?"

Hesitantly, she took it and looked inside. The envelope contained multiple papers. "What is this?"

"It's the deed. I bought it, and now it's yours."

"Are you serious?"

"You should know by now that I don't have a good sense of humor," he said with a chuckle. "But I am serious."

"I can't accept this. You know I wanted to do it myself."

"You wouldn't take the money. You wouldn't keep the ring. Accept the help. I got it away from Thomas for you. My lawyer is waiting for us to arrive at her office so I can sign it all over to you."

"I can't pay you right now."

"I don't want anything for it."

"Why?"

"For the same reason you helped me. Because I like you. And no matter what happened between us, I want to be your friend. Friends help each other. He was charging you a ridiculous amount for this place. I even managed to get it for cheaper."

"Why would Thomas sell to you?"

"I did it anonymously through my lawyers. If you're worried about accepting the money, consider it an investment." He paused. "And I wanted to apologize. I acted like a horse's ass. I shouldn't have talked to you like that. I was angry at myself, and I lashed out."

"I did too. I'm truly sorry." Earlier that day, she'd thought her life had spiraled down around her. But finding out that Garrett now owned the property she'd spent her entire adult life dreaming about, and that he was willing to sign the deed over to her—she couldn't believe it. Willa's life had never worked out that way. She'd wanted the independence to do it herself, but there was nothing wrong with her accepting help from a friend. "Thank you."

He smiled. "Great. Let's get to my lawyer's office. Get in, I'll drive."

He started for the truck, but she didn't move. He'd done this to help her. There was no reason why she couldn't help him out. "Wait, Garrett."

He turned. "Yeah?"

"I'll do it. I'll marry you."

"Really?"

"Of course."

"What made you change your mind?"

"I… I'm in love with you."

He paused. "Willa."

"I think that's been my problem this whole time. I was so afraid of falling in love with you that I pushed you away. So many times."

"You're in love with me." He said it as a statement, not a question. She nodded. "Thank God," he said, drawing her in for a kiss. He pulled back. "I love you too."

Seventeen

Six months later

Garrett held Willa's hand as he slid the white-gold-and-diamond ring over her fourth finger. "Do you, Garrett, take Willa to be your wife?" the officiant asked him.

"I do."

"Willa, do you take Garrett to be your husband?"

After reconciling, they'd decided that they wanted to get married as soon as possible.

For their wedding venue, they'd selected the isolated stream where they'd first made love under the stars. Unknown to the few friends and family gathered, the altar was set up where they'd lain on an old blanket, drinking strawberry wine.

"I do."

"I now pronounce you—"

"Wait," Garrett said, interrupting. "I have something to say."

Willa stiffened. That was exactly how she had ended her first wedding. Startled gasps rang out in the small congregation as everyone—including Willa—wondered if he was ending it. Was he coming clean with the charade? Was she getting karmic retribution?

"Willa, I didn't know when we first met that you were the one for me." He smiled. "Of course, we were only kids at the time." There were chuckles from the small group as the tension faded. "It may have taken a while, but I knew that you were the one I wanted to marry—for real, this time." More laughter. "But the past six months have been the most incredible in my life. You showed me that there is more to life than work." She knew his words were from the heart. Those weren't his prepared vows. This declaration was not an act. "I want to keep learning that lesson from you for the rest of my life. I love you."

He'd said those words to her before. But this time, she knew it was real. "I know that I was reluctant at first," she told him. "I've been closed off. But you forced me out of my comfort zone and made me realize there was so much to be happy about. I love you too."

The officiant cleared his throat. "If that's everything," he said with a smile, "I'd like to finally pronounce you husband and wife. You may now kiss each other."

Garrett pulled Willa to him and dipped her for their first kiss as a married couple. This had all started as a charade, a sham relationship; but as they broke apart, Willa looked up into the eyes of her husband. She was madly in love with him, and there was nothing fake about it.

Eighteen

After the ceremony, and after pictures were taken, Garrett slipped into his grandfather's study. He needed to take a moment away from the craziness of the day. He'd thought that having a small wedding would mean an easier, quieter day. Between greeting guests, making sure the details were right and confessing his undying love for Willa, that had not been the case. While she was changing into her reception dress, he wanted to take advantage of a moment of solitude. He reached for the Macallan bottle that Elias hadn't managed to hide well enough from him. His solitude was short-lived, however, when the door opened behind him. He turned and saw it was his grandfather.

"I knew I'd find you getting into the good stuff."

Garrett laughed and poured a glass and passed it to his grandfather. Gently, they clinked their glasses together and drank in silence.

When Elias lowered his glass, he had a grin on his face. "I've got a confession to make, Garrett."

"What's that?"

"I knew from the beginning that your relationship with Willa was a sham."

Garrett stiffened. "I'm embarrassed about how that all went down. I should have known better."

Elias held up a hand, cutting him off. "I'm not stupid. Or blind. But I was willing to let you ride it out. I was waiting for you to cut and run. But you didn't. And when your arrangement fell apart, I thought that you would fight for the ranch. Take me to court, have me deemed legally incompetent."

"It's not too late for that, is it?" he joked.

Elias ignored the remark. "But in the end, your relationship wasn't a sham, was it?"

"No. I love her so much. And I have you to thank for pushing me outside of my comfort zone. I'm sorry for lying. But I couldn't risk the fact that you were going to turn the place over to anyone else."

"Neither of them would ever get this place. I love your brothers. But they've never wanted this kind of life. Not even controlling interest of the ranch would bring them back here."

"If you busted me for trying to have a sham wedding, who's getting the ranch?"

"You really are dumber than a boot. It was *always* going to be you, you dumbass."

"So, all of this…"

"Was as phony as the beginning of your relationship with Willa. How did you get her on board? Offer her money? But as the months went on, I could see the difference between you. You got closer. I could tell you loved each other. And I'm glad you finally see it. You really love each other, don't you?"

"It took us a while to get there, but yeah, we do. No regrets. We'll be happy together."

"And that's all I wanted for you." He patted his grandson on the shoulder before leaving him with his thoughts.

Again, just like at Elias's engagement party, Garrett was left alone in his grandfather's study. He thought about how his life had changed since then. There was a knock on the door. It opened, and his new bride came in.

"Hi, husband."

"Hello, wife."

"Everything okay with your grandfather?"

"Yeah. Apparently, our act wasn't as convincing as we thought it was." He told her about his grandfather's thoughts.

"Is everything okay between you, though? Do you still get what you want?"

He took her hands and pulled her closer. "I already have what I want. What I need."

"And the ranch?"

"It was always mine. This was all 'faker than the beginning of our relationship.' My grandfather's words."

"So, we didn't need to do any of this?"

"I'm glad we did, though. I'm glad he made the ultimatum. It forced me to get out of my comfort zone. To take a chance on love."

"Me too."

He could hear the music starting on the other side of the door. "It's time for our first dance."

"I kind of want to stay here for a little while longer."

He took out his cell phone and cued up the same old country song that they'd first danced to at Daisy's g⸺ the one that they'd selected for their first dance as a married couple. "We've spent our entire relationship doing things for people to see. Why don't we take this moment alone? Would you like to dance, Mrs. Hardwell?"

She put her hand in his. "We'll discuss the surname thing later," she told him. "But for now, let's dance."

* * * * *

WE HOPE YOU ENJOYED
THIS BOOK FROM

DESIRE

*Luxury, scandal, desire—welcome to
the lives of the American elite.*

Be transported to the worlds of oil barons, family dynasties,
moguls and celebrities. Get ready for juicy plot twists,
delicious sensuality and intriguing scandal.

6 NEW BOOKS AVAILABLE EVERY MONTH!

"There's no need to insult me, Cambria. After all, we'll
be seeing a lot of each other over the next two weeks."

"Oh, I see. You're the type that can dish it, but can't
take it. Ain't that something?" she scoffed, then shook her
head. "Let's make a deal—I'll show you the same level
of respect you show me." She grabbed her handbag from
the table. "So remember the next time you open your
mouth, you can expect me to match whatever energy you
throw out."

HDEXP0822

He watched her, silently surveying the way her glossy lips pursed into a straight line, the defiant tilt of her chin, the challenge in her eyes. She was mesmerizing, disconcerting even. No woman had ever affected him this way before. *She knocks me so off balance, but for some reason, I like it.*

Her lips parted. "Why are you staring at me like that?"

Don't miss what happens next in...
What Happens After Hours
by Kianna Alexander.

Available October 2022 wherever
Harlequin Desire books and ebooks are sold.

Harlequin.com

Get 4 FREE REWARDS!

We'll send you 2 FREE Books plus 2 FREE Mystery Gifts.

FREE
Value Over
$20

Both the **Harlequin® Desire** and **Harlequin Presents®** series feature compelling novels filled with passion, sensuality and intriguing scandals.

YES! Please send me 2 FREE novels from the Harlequin Desire or Harlequin Presents series and my 2 FREE gifts (gifts are worth about $10 retail). After receiving them, if I don't wish to receive any more books, I can return the shipping statement marked "cancel." If I don't cancel, I will receive 6 brand-new Harlequin Presents Larger-Print books every month and be billed just $6.05 each in the U.S. or $6.24 each in Canada, a savings of at least 10% off the cover price or 6 Harlequin Desire books every month and be billed just $4.80 each in the U.S. and $5.49 each in Canada, a savings of at least 13% off the cover price. It's quite a bargain! Shipping and handling is just 50¢ per book in the U.S. and $1.25 per book in Canada.* I understand that accepting the 2 free books and gifts places me under no obligation to buy anything. I can always return a shipment and cancel at any time by calling the number below. The free books and gifts are mine to keep no matter what I decide.

Choose one: ☐ **Harlequin Desire**
(225/326 HDN GRTW)

☐ **Harlequin Presents Larger-Print**
(176/376 HDN GQ9Z)

Name (please print)

Address   Apt. #

City   State/Province   Zip/Postal Code

Email: Please check this box ☐ if you would like to receive newsletters and promotional emails from Harlequin Enterprises ULC and its affiliates. You can unsubscribe anytime.

Mail to the **Harlequin Reader Service:**
IN U.S.A.: P.O. Box 1341, Buffalo, NY 14240-8531
IN CANADA: P.O. Box 603, Fort Erie, Ontario L2A 5X3

Want to try 2 free books from another series! Call **1-800-873-8635** or visit www.ReaderService.com.

*Terms and prices subject to change without notice. Prices do not include sales taxes, which will be charged (if applicable) based on your state or country of residence. Canadian residents will be charged applicable taxes. Offer not valid in Quebec. This offer is limited to one order per household. Books received may not be as shown. Not valid for current subscribers to the Harlequin Presents or Harlequin Desire series. All orders subject to approval. Credit or debit balances in a customer's account(s) may be offset by any other outstanding balance owed by or to the customer. Please allow 4 to 6 weeks for delivery. Offer available while quantities last.

Your Privacy—Your information is being collected by Harlequin Enterprises ULC, operating as Harlequin Reader Service. For a complete summary of the information we collect, how we use this information and to whom it is disclosed, please visit our privacy notice located at corporate.harlequin.com/privacy-notice. From time to time we may also exchange your personal information with reputable third parties. If you wish to opt out of this sharing of your personal information, please visit readerservice.com/consumerschoice or call 1-800-873-8635. **Notice to California Residents**—Under California law, you have specific rights to control and access your data. For more information on these rights and how to exercise them, visit corporate.harlequin.com/california-privacy.

HDHP22R2